IMMORTAL WOUND

Gail P. Robertson

Immortal Wound

ISBN: 978-0-9921203-9-9

ACKNOWLEDGEMENTS

This novel is dedicated to my beloved late husband, Pete Robertson, for all his encouragement and the suggestion to create a novel around selected dialogues I recorded in parahypnotic 'levels'.

Special thanks to my dear friend Alan Stibbard, who introduced me to the technique. Without his patient tutelage and mentoring, this story – and likely this writer – would not be here.

Immortal Wound Cover:

The cover art consists of elements from five photographs, the use of which I purchased from Shutterstock and then modified to create the cover.

PREFACE

This metaphysical tale takes place both on Earth and in the 'native realm' where we might in fact reside. Though the book is fictional, the basic premise may include elements of reality.

I suspect we timespacers project our focus into virtual realities conceived to let us explore the 'What happens when . . .? of our not-yet-understanding'. Before doing so, we choose the era, location and main theme(s) for our lifetime. Once on-site, though, we can make any changes we want; we have full say.

Some timespacers think to 'call home' and ask those questions uppermost on our minds. I call the responders 'Helpliners'.

My hypnosis instructor, Alan Stibbard, introduced me to the technique of 'calling home' on March 3, 1985. Since then, I have recorded all conversations done that way, and have liberally infused select passages into this story. The perspectives played a huge role in my maturation process. I can hope that perhaps they will be of use as well to you, the reader.

Please enjoy . . .

Gail P. Robertson

NATIVE REALM
CHARACTERS

when and where they first appear

IMMORTAL WOUND

CHAPTER 1

Location: Non-timespacial Native
Realm

Helpliner Cool Pastel tensed as the
growing unease of his workmates
impinged on his aura. He had been holding
back, traversing as slowly as possible,
without being obvious about it, the void of
nonspace that separated the Helpline arc of
semi-recliners from the Debriefing site.
His fellow light beings had already
arranged themselves in a fair semblance of
being seated on three of the five plush
chairs surrounding an oval ebony table.
Pastel unobtrusively slipped onto his own
chair and waited apprehensively.

They were completely alone in this
region of nonspace. The psyches who
managed the Native Realm had set this
expanse aside for the Helpliners' exclusive
use and kept it scrupulously separate, it

being the single point of contact with those who were timespacing.

What did I say wrong this time? Pastel fretted. His mind rifled through the calls he had answered from the outfocused during that shift. It was scarcely the first time he'd messed up, but surely . . . .

Pastel glanced at Soft Murmur on his left. If she was annoyed with him, she was hiding it well. The distressing silence made Pastel twitch inwardly. He was casting around for something to say – anything that would give him a clue as to what he'd done, when Sweet Memory blurted out, "Is it true, then? About Beacon Tower?"

The team's newest member was a timid soul, easily flustered. Her normally milky-white essence was awash with muddy browns and slashes of yellowish-greens.

Murmur projected a nod. "I'm afraid so. It's a real shame, too; he was approaching elderhood. Now . . ." She approximated a humanesque sigh.

"What about him?" Pastel asked at once, relieved to not be the cause of their discomfiture.

Silent Echo, on Memory's left, radiated surprise. "I thought you would have heard.

You remember Brock? He was the 18th-century American butler?"

"Yeah, he called here a few times. But we haven't heard from him in – what? It must be decades . . . his time," Pastel hastened to add.

"No, and neither have the other teams," Echo confirmed before Pastel could ask. Helpline Teams 1 through 4 monitored the human frequencies in shifts, assisting those timespacers who thought to 'call home'.

"Brock was fixated on his employers' welfare, paying little attention to his own. Utterly devoted," Echo explained for Memory's benefit, before returning his focus to Pastel. "He was due back two shifts ago and never arrived. Turns out, he locked himself to the mansion when his body died. Beacon Tower was running that lifetime. Ever meet him?"

Pastel felt his essence constrict. "No. He's on Team 4, that's all I know. But we've all lost at least one focus –."

"He was running three this time, and since he had developed so much energy, he'd infused a lot into his focuses. Both the others also stayed behind. Brock was the last." A shudder ran through Echo's essence, reminding Pastel of a miniscule earthquake.

"Must've been quite a shock. I mean, that sort of wholesale defection hasn't happened in . . ."

"Eons," Echo stated. "But it's always a risk."

Which was true, though Pastel had never given it much thought. "How's Tower taking it?"

"Pretty hard, I hear. He's diminished. Permanently."

Memory recoiled. "But that's not possible! Once the mansion falls, and whatever his other focuses globbed onto disintegrates, they'll return, right?"

"By then, it'll be too late," Murmur explained. "All Tower will get back is a fraction of the energy and focus he invested. The rest will have radiated off into the time-space environment, along with the minute-to-minute memories his entities had amassed."

Memory gawked at Murmur. "But how can that *be*? Time-space isn't even real; it's just a mind-game. How could Tower leave part of himself there when he never left here?"

4

"Time-space isn't real but core energy is, and it fuels all virtual realities. That includes the bodies our outfocused grow," Murmur reminded her. "Thing is, Tower can't sustain Brock or the others without a body to focus on. Every time they manifest – and even in between, though not as much – they draw from their reserves with reduced opportunities to replenish them. But don't worry." Pastel detected the calming reassurance Murmur was covertly directing at Memory. "Tower is strong; he'll be alright. He has plenty of friends to help him adjust. And eventually, if he applies himself, he could increase his mass to almost make up for what he lost."

The black edges that had begun to surround Memory's aura muted noticeably. "So . . ."

"So who is Zephyr talking to? Anyone catch it?", Pastel asked, more to change the subject and reduce the pall that had settled over them than out of actual interest. Their elder and shift leader had taken a call just before the stint ended.

The others pounced on the new topic, speculating freely. Almost immediately, tensions plummeted. Pastel covertly gazed at Murmur, loving her even more for her compassion towards Memory. At length, Murmur's focus strayed in his direction and he looked away, afraid his feelings would betray him.

Murmur was fast-tracking towards elderhood. Pastel grimly reminded himself that he was the last thing she needed in her way. The thought gave him no solace, for Murmur was his one forever love. He had adored her from the moment they met.

Until now, pale time-space romances had sustained him, easing the loneliness which gnawed at him relentlessly. But Pastel had just taken the last trip to which he was entitled. He would spend the equivalent of the next billion years confined to the Native Realm. Without love. Ever.

Inside, his soul wailed piteously, railing against the sentence it could not, would not accept.

Not now! Pastel thought desperately. He barely managed to wrestle the pain of it into submission before it could manifest in his aura, where the others would surely notice. *I'll find another outlet,* he promised himself bleakly. *I have to.*

He was distracted by the sudden appearance of an orb of light, larger than the others already seated there. The being positioned himself on the remaining chair at the head of the table. The debriefing could now begin.

And not a moment too soon, Pastel thought.

"Sorry to keep you," Zephyr said briskly. "Who's first?"

"Me," Pastel volunteered, desperate to escape the turmoil uppermost in his mind. He produced a psychic recorder and extruded a pseudo-finger to hover above the activation point. "It was Open Mind, who is timespacing as Ricky, the alcoholic. North America, circa 1933 Gregorian."

"How's it – I mean, *he* – doing?"

Zephyr still tended to refer to the outfocused as they really were, rather than by the gender the timespacing portion had assumed. That, and the Helpliners assigning themselves names, had been Pastel's latest ideas. Even Zephyr had noticed a deeper empathy from Team 1 members towards their callers through emulating the human experience. Pastel especially enjoyed the challenge of conversing in words rather than the effortless perception of shared thoughts.

"Ricky's still trying to dry out. He'd been hallucinating pretty badly. I was keeping watch so he wouldn't harm himself. As you know, he's nowhere near finished that lifetime. Anyway, for a moment my thoughts wandered." Pastel cast a guilty glance in Murmur's direction, and hoped she wouldn't think less of him for the lapse. "I was wondering how Ricky might react if he knew he wasn't alone. And you know what he did? He looked wildly around the room and hollered, 'Wha'dya mean, I ain't alone?'"

Even Zephyr leaned forward, his focus becoming laser-thin and aimed directly at Pastel. It was all the Helpliner could do not to squirm as he continued his report.

"It could have been a coincidence," Pastel admitted. "I mean, he was seeing a lot of things that weren't there – not even in a time-space sense. 'Ricky!' I said, pouring *urgency* into my mental voice. 'Can you hear me? I'm your monitor.' He looked up (don't they all?) and said, 'What's a monitor?'"

"So he *did* hear you. Excellent." Zephyr projected a smile and relaxed backward a micron. "Go on."

"We talked. He asked the usual are-you-God-or-an-angel sort of questions. He was having no trouble at all 'hearing' me. Anyway, after a bit he said, 'Hey, tell me somethin': In these here flophouses an' them soup kitchens, they keep harpin' at us to 'seek the truth'. So I wanna know: What *is* 'the truth'?"

"Woah! What did you tell him?" Silent Echo took advantage of the near-Earth-equivalent gravity that the Debriefing site had been allotted to sprout elbows and lean on the table.

"Well, I started small, of course; he was in pretty rough shape. But here, listen for yourself." Pastel triggered the recorder.

. . . So I wanna know: What *is* 'the truth'?

Ah, yes, 'the one and only truth'. Everyone has their own idea of what that is, but in fact, *you* decide. Let me put it this way: Humans can't fly; that's the truth. But you really wanted to. So, though wingless, you *decided* to fly anyway, and proceeded to devise a way. The moment you succeeded, *that truth became false.* You *made* it false, and made what you wanted, true. You can either live out your truths, or your decisions; the choice is yours.

Pastel froze the recording to interject, "There – that sound you heard? That was him plopping down on his cot." He let the machine continue.

So yer sayin' there ain't no such thing as 'the truth'? All I gotta do is build me one that'll let me do anythin' I want?

Pastel watched his teammates exchange knowing glances. Ricky had jumped to one of the most dangerous conclusions a timespacer could. Most Helpliners made that mistake during one excursion or another, and some (like Pastel) had done so numerous times.

Oh, no, Ricky; don't do that! Only hold to it so long as it serves your purposes. Never let a truth govern you, for doing so is like building a statue and then becoming its slave. The statue can do nothing more than be a statue. But you can perceive it as restricting or controlling you and how you live your life. That's a trap many people fall into. They use a limiting truth or belief to make them feel powerless in an area and not take responsibility for that decision.

Ya mean like that I can't stop drinkin', 'cause I keep fallin' off the wagon. But what if I really can't quit? That wouldn't be no truth; that'd be a *fact*.

Would it, Ricky? A truth speaks, not for itself, but for you. It says what *you* tell it to say, to yourself and others. Which also means, it speaks about you. What do you want your truth to say?

The recorder cycled through a lengthy silence.

Ricky?

Yeah?

You might want to make notes.

My hand's shakin'. I can't write when my hand's shakin'.

Is that your truth?

A sheepish laugh emanated from the recorder.

Nah, I'll get it down somehow. (Pause) Ya comin' back?

Do you want me to?

Yeah, I guess I do.

Alright, I will. And you can 'call' me, too, if you want. Here's how . . . .

Pastel stopped the recorder and waited expectantly.

"That was a cusp; I'm sure of it," Echo said. "I could hear it in his voice."

"I think so, too," Pastel agreed. And if Ricky was determined to break his addiction, Pastel would seed opportunities to help him do so. "Any suggestions, Zephyr?"

"Let him do as much as possible on his own. Answer his questions, but don't give him a hand unless he really needs it. I can't reinforce this enough, people." The shift elder raised his 'voice' a tad. "Don't get caught up in their appearances. Remember who they really are – our colleagues – and why they chose these experiences. Open Mind is only *playing* Ricky the alcoholic, remember. He will not be pleased if we interfere unnecessarily in his game. He *likes* big challenges; that's why he chooses these scenarios to get embroiled in."

Zephyr tapped the table surface and said thoughtfully, "The Ricky persona was planning a rude awakening for himself after he hit rock-bottom, wasn't he?"

Pastel consulted Open Mind's 'flight plan', the main-event outline a traveler logged before outfocusing. "Yes. He was to be injured by a car while staggering crossing the road. He might not have to now."

"Keep a close eye on him," Zephyr addressed the group. "If he pulls himself out of this on his own, we can throw away the script. He – and we – will be 'winging it' from there on in. And remember, we're not allowed to skip ahead to find out what happens. If he slipstreams into an ad-lib lifetime, we play the game by his rules. Understand?"

The assemblage nodded dutifully. Pastel felt an electric surge of anticipation. Those were the most exciting and unpredictable lifetimes, but they were tricky to monitor.

Too bad I can't pull a stunt like that on Open Mind's watch, Pastel thought, and felt his mood instantly flatten. Having to experience time-space vicariously through his callers was a poor substitute for the real thing, but it was the only option left. He resolved to sit extra shifts on the other Teams. At least that would minimize the time he'd be alone with his thoughts.

"Who's next?" Zephyr eyed the others.

Murmur produced a credible throat-clearing sound which drew smiles of approval. "Safe Haven as Peter, the therapist – Austria, circa 2170 – had another insightful question." She activated her own recorder.

How can I explain to my clients that self-discipline is only meant to guide, not to shackle or confine?

Murmur paused the mechanism to say, "What was foremost on his mind was, 'Why are some of my clients who are really trying hard, failing?'. Here's what I told him:

Self-discipline is not a jailer. You can perceive a door as ensuring your privacy or as locking you in. But it is your door, with the lock on your side. You decide what role it will play for you.

The problem some of your clients are having is that they don't work out beforehand what their goal entails.

Before they even start, they should decide what action they're going to take, the sequence of events, the time frame involved, who the participants will be, and so on. Because they don't do that, they've no idea how to proceed. Without this necessary pre-thinking, and then using the details as tools to get the job done, all they have are the decision and the end result, with nothing in between to bridge the gap. So they thrash around, not getting very far.

That's when they get frustrated and blame themselves for lack of self-discipline, instead of for not having preplanned. Or, if they *do* keep at their goal, they try to smash through the obstacles without the means in hand to succeed. They feel overwhelmed by the effort and energy they're having to apply to make even minimal progress. You might want to remind them: *You must work twice as hard when you have only half the tools.*"

Memory stopped the recital. "The rest was just curiosity about our hobbies and personal goals. He was in a chatty mood."

"Speaking of hobbies," Pastel said. "I checked with Wise Acre, aka Cindy, the sage. Switzerland, 1795. She has penned more of those nifty aphorisms of hers. I recorded them, of course. If anyone wants a copy*, let me know. I think we'll be hearing from her again soon. She was guarding her thoughts and feelings, so I think she wants to consider something 'in private' before discussing it with us."

Zephyr projected a nod. "It's her right, so no prying till she's ready. How about you, Echo? Anything you want to tell us?"

Echo's aura took on a sheepish pink glow. "You were answering a call right then. I'm surprised you heard."

"Not much. Which is why I want to review it now."

"Who was it?" Memory asked.

Echo sighed. "Twisted Humor, aka Gail, the writer. Of course, she's not one yet. As you know, she's still in her 'being a loner' stage. Anyway, I decided to play a little hardball with her."

* excerpts from Pastel's notes begin on page 341.

For once, location and era were left out. Each team member had fielded so many of her queries – sometimes thrice in a shift and often on trifling issues – that she needed no introduction.

Still, she is coming along fairly well, based on her purposes for the trip, Pastel reminded himself charitably.

"At this point, Gail is still deathly afraid of becoming emotionally trapped in a relationship," Echo explained, directing his comment at Memory.

Pastel suspected Echo was stalling for time. He himself had used that ploy more than once, while he considered the best spin to put on his actions.

"But her loneliness is crippling her," Echo continued. "I know you said to handle her with care, Zephyr, but I took a chance and I think it paid off."

Echo triggered his recorder.

Can you identify what is coming between me and my ability to make goals?

You fear the goals you would have, but for the fear.

"You were baiting her," Zephyr stated. His 'voice' was carefully neutral, but

Pastel thought he detected a hint of censure.

"Guiding her, mostly," Echo hedged. He let the recording continue.

Can you tell me what those goals would be?

You long to find your soulmate and have a family.

WHAT? No! Never! That's the one thing I *don't* want; you *know* that.

Gail, each focus has its own loves and fears, and its own problems to solve. Work to resolve your fears and old associations on this and other topics, then put in fresh, intelligent guidelines. The topic isn't at fault; the associations are. Remember, if you are afraid of a topic, it means that topic has an attraction or meaning for you. Otherwise it would not be a factor, and you'd have erased it from your mind and life long ago.

That hurts!

It only hurts because you are afraid to tackle and resolve the problem for fear there will then be nothing to keep that future at bay. Courage is needed, and trust that we counsel you from a broader understanding in that area than you have at your time-space level. Understanding is our strength, but doing is yours, held in awful check by your many fears. Get them out of the way; they are killing your drive.

For a long time, there was silence on the recorder.

How do I do that? (The voice was tense, dread etched in every word.)

Use your logic –

"She's always trying to be logical, so I figured I'd use that as an 'in'," Echo interjected.

You already know that you set the guidelines of your experience in any area of your life, having done so many times in positive ways and countless times to your detriment. You also know you're always in control, and that you are never really damaged by your experiences. And if that isn't enough, you have highly supportive friends who would not let you make a serious mistake. Add to that the fact that we would never let you go in a self-destructive direction, either – not after all the progress you've made – and you tell me: What could generate so much fear except old associations which no longer apply? Break the illusion, Gail. When you perceive the present through the eyes of the past, you are living in a false world, a hallucination. *Wake up!*

A subtle fluctuation in Zephyr's cream-colored aura told Pastel their leader had split his focus. Presently it stabilized.

"I just checked on her. She *is* thinking more clearly, and for once, keeping her anxieties in check." Zephyr's projection became stern. "I think you made the right call. This time. But be very careful. Tactics like that can backfire disastrously."

"I was monitoring her emotions. If she'd truly panicked, I would have calmed her and then backed off," was Echo's defensive reply.

"Alright. Anything more any of you wants to discuss? No? Adjourned."

*

The others wandered off, and Pastel went in search of company. The choice wasn't difficult; he had only one close friend. Whisper (as Pastel called the Life Properties Infuser) was intimately involved with a solar system deep inside what humans called the Milky Way. To telepathic beings, names were unnecessary, but like most occasional timespacers, Whisper didn't seem to mind the pseudonym Pastel gave him. Whisper's public mind had just shrugged it off as yet another harmless Helpliner quirk.

Pastel touched his friend's presence and was instantly there. "Looks like you're just about ready," Pastel noted, switching his mental view to a close-up of the third planet circling the teenage sun. An ancient supernova had produced the raw material which eventually spawned this current grouping.

"I was just about to nudge it – here, here, here and here." Whisper's thought-feelings vibrated eagerly. "That 'soup' is just right for mobile life forms."

"What are you seeding this time? Silicon or carbon-based?"

"Germanium." Whisper was silent for a moment as he marginally increased the temperature of the hot springs flanking one of the sites. "I think it'll do well, especially since there are no methane-breathers close by to interfere with its evolution."

"This will be your first time using germanium as a base, won't it?" Pastel stared at the first pond. The seeding of life properties never ceased to impress him.

"Yes. I've been working up to it slowly. You can't rush these things. One small oversight can ruin the fragile balance and the spark dies. Then you have to reset the environment and start all over again." Whisper flexed his aura in anticipation. "Okay, I'm ready."

Pastel felt the mental change as his friend marshaled his focus into a sharp lance of conscious energy, pinpointing in turn each of the four ponds. Pastel tried to perceptually slow down that moment of transformation from empty to 'occupied', but as always the conversion occurred too quickly. Without realizing it, Pastel sighed.

"Just come off shift, I see," Whisper remarked, leaking satisfaction over his handiwork. Pastel knew the nursers would soon take over, to patiently monitor the new life forms in an accelerated perception of the crucial first few dozen millennia. That would free up Whisper to find another celestial body ready to accept life. Until the nursers arrived, though, Whisper would oversee his 'kids', reveling in the illusion of parenthood. Envy stabbed and Pastel muted it, but not quickly enough.

"You could do it, too, you know," Whisper reminded him for the umpteenth time. "Just say the word. Our elder keeps complaining we don't have enough staff. He'd snap you up in an instant. Besides, admit it, you could use a change. You've been answering those same old inane timespacer questions for – how long now?"

"You didn't consider *your* questions so inane last time out, when you finally got around to calling us," Pastel shot back, sidestepping his friend's pointed question. "You're lucky we Helpliners are a patient lot. Remember the trouble you'd gotten yourself into? What if you'd called and no one bothered to answer?"

Whisper shuddered. "Don't even say that! But seriously, think about it. The Helpline has plenty of volunteers. It's not like they'd be hurting if you transferred. And you can't deny you get a thrill out of watching me do this. You always show up just before the Big Event."

"Someday, maybe."

Two calm nurturing presences appeared beside them, and Pastel added his greeting to Whisper's before asking his friend, "Care for an exer-game?" He needed to stretch himself after a long stint on the Helpline, but it was no fun doing it alone.

"Sure. But let's see if –" The LPI projected the personality-print of his mate, who Pastel had dubbed Sirene. "– is finished her practicum. She's learning how to seal the dividing line between that new universe (I think you call it 'Universe L') and its antimatter counterpart."

"How does Sirene get such juicy projects?" To Pastel it sounded deliciously dangerous.

"Dunno. I'd've grabbed it myself if I hadn't been so busy."

The subtle dig wasn't lost on Pastel, but he ignored it.

The trio spent most of their free-range breaks together, as they had similar tastes in entertainment. Whisper contacted his forever mate, who promptly joined them.

"Your arrival freshens our midst like an ocean breeze," Pastel proclaimed, hoping she would enjoy the sensory output he was projecting.

Sirene wriggled in pleasure. "Ooh! Thank you. That felt tingly!"

"My pleasure."

"Excuse us a moment, would you? Hi, honey." Without waiting for Pastel to respond, Sirene stepped into Whisper to blend in a communion of oneness. As they merged, a tiny supernova of contained energy flared, bathing Pastel in radiant joy. He opened wide to drink in their reflected bliss, and in that unprotected moment, knew implicitly that it was the closest he would ever come to experiencing true love.

NOOOOOO! His essence screamed, writhing.

Not now! Pastel mentally hissed at himself.

From deep within, the starving ache begged to be heard. The need was so overwhelming that Pastel almost gasped. He glanced at his friends and ruthlessly subsumed the anguish, all the while hoping desperately his friends' preoccupation with each other had kept them from learning his secret. Pastel fought to gain control of his auric shades and return them to a more neutral tone.

Presently, the lovers' energy patterns separated.

"So, Sirene, how did the practicum go?" Pastel asked quickly, mostly to distract them from noticing any telltale color residues. Of course, during their union, Whisper would have experienced Sirene's practicum in detail, but Pastel wasn't privy to such intimacy.

"My instructor was impressed, but I should have done better. Why is it I only realize my mistakes *afterwards*?" Shafts of red exasperation marred her normally serene essence.

Whisper playfully bumped her. "I've a better question: Why do you always expect perfection from yourself?"

"What is that Earth expression you told me?" Sirene turned toward Pastel.

"You mean, 'I want it all, and I want it now'?"

"Yes, that's the one. And I *do*."

Whisper vibrated with mirth. "You and everyone else! So, what's your pleasure, love?"

"Something active. I've been stationary too long."

"Streak, perhaps?" Pastel ventured.

"I could go that."

Pastel constricted slightly. "I'm a bit out of practice. Will you spot me one?"

"Sure," Sirene and Whisper said in unison.

"Then you're on!" Pastel stretched himself out into a laser-thin stream of incandescent blue light and rocketed across nonspace.

"Cheater!" Sirene belatedly snaked out a long 'arm' to snag him, but he was already out of reach.

"You said you'd spot me one. That was it." Pastel used his explosion of kinetic energy to build up a charge of glee. The sensation was a wonderful reprieve from the feelings he had just endured, and Pastel reveled in them. The emotional thrust also gave him sufficient speed to safely outdistance their promontories.

"Catch me if you can," Pastel taunted, doubling back to tease them. Other souls stopped to watch the game. He ignored the strategies some of them beamed to him. Others, he knew, were sending his opponents their own pet tactics.

But Pastel knew exactly what to do to keep one step ahead of his competition. Every time his friends closed in, Pastel arced crazily, waiting till the last instant to make good his escape.

Finally, he egged them a moment too long.

"GOTCHA!" Whisper cried, lassoing Pastel with his aura. The essence spread out in all directions to enclose him.

In the white-hot need to escape, to *win* at all costs, Pastel blasted his essence in two. Whisper's trap closed around nothing.

Whisper gawked. "How'd you do that?"

But Pastel now had an unexpected problem: how to reintegrate his essence. Unable to direct either half, he could only watch in alarm as the two segments flew ever further apart.

"HELP!" Pastel shouted, panicking.

Promptly, his twin pieces stopped their headlong flight. Pastel felt them being herded together. Within moments, they touched and merged.

"Before you split again, I want you in our element for training."

Pastel didn't have to ask who his rescuer was. Only a psyche exuded that much mental force. He flushed in embarrassment. "Thank you. I'm sorry I bothered you."

"You bothered you more," was the powerhouse's good-naturedly reply, before it disappeared back into its 'hallowed domain'. Or so Pastel had always imagined that region, having never been there. His feelings quickened at the thought of not just visiting the psyches' locale, but actually being taught by one.

Whisper pulled up alongside Pastel. "How did you do that?" he repeated.

"I haven't a clue. I just . . ." Pastel stopped, not at all sure exactly *what* he had done.

"Impressive. I thought only psyches could split like that."

Pastel winced. "Apparently not."

"And you will get to be trained." Sirene moaned wistfully.

"Just in that one teensy area. You're the one who's on track to become a psyche some day." The thought humbled Pastel more than he cared to admit.

Sirene sighed. "Not for ages. I'm not even an elder yet." Then her gaze turned pointedly toward Whisper. "I think I've had enough exer-excitement for now, if you don't mind."

"Me, too." Whisper migrated closer to Sirene.

Pastel could take a hint if it was broad enough. "I'd better brush up on splitting. See you guys later."

As their presences winked away, Pastel mentally accessed whatever the communal memory library held on 'doing the splits'.

CHAPTER 2

"Echo, if you aren't too busy . . ." Pastel transmitted, when he had exhausted the library's meager offerings on the subject.

"No, I'm free."

He found Silent Echo contemplating a temporal scene, a panoramic view of a cluster of small universes. Pastel perched himself on the ledge Echo had materialized and now obligingly extended for Pastel.

"I thought you'd be *helping* Whisper."

Pastel's coloring deepened at the pointed reminder of how he had overstated his involvement in Whisper's work the shift before. He hadn't meant to deceive; it had slipped out somehow.

"Just wishful thinking, inadvertently verbalized," Pastel said mendaciously. "But listen . . . I'm wondering about the jolt you gave Gail. Did she go looking for her soulmate yet?" Pastel could easily have checked for himself, but since Echo had gone out on a professional limb for this timespacer, it seemed only fair to ask him instead.

"I checked on her a couple years later, and she still hadn't, though her fear level had markedly decreased. But I'm planning a little surprise for her. I'll schedule it for about a year from my 'jolt', as you call it, so she won't make the connection."

"Oh? What have you got in mind?" Pastel interest sharpened. Echo was well known for his unconventional methods. It was one of the things Pastel liked about him.

"She does this little 'experiential' expansion thing. She imagines a tunnel leading to a meadow inside a collapsed mountain top, with a stream down the right side and a waterfall in the distance. Thing is, the only parameter she put in is that she'll learn something in there she needs to know." Echo paused significantly. "Also, her soulmate spends a lot of time in reverie. I'm going to have them meet in that 'meadow'."

"I like."

Echo nodded. "There's more than one way to trounce a fear. She feels safe in there, so her shields are down. Of course, I'll be monitoring."

"Naturally." Pastel tried to recall exact dates from Gail's 'flight plan'. "When does she meet her soulmate in the flesh?"

"Not for another six of her years. But this shared experience will make a good base for when they do meet."

Pastel regarded his colleague with admiration. "Wish I had your talent for sneakiness."

"Why not develop it next time you –. Sorry; I forgot, you can't."

Pastel felt like a damp sheen was forming on his aura. "Say, you wouldn't spot me a lifetime, would you? I could sit extra shifts, leave you free to spend more time on that side project I hear you've got."

Echo didn't back away from Pastel, but that was the impression he gave. "I don't think that's a good idea. What you really need is a hobby, something *here* you can get into."

Pastel *was* sweating, he was sure of it. "But there's so much more I could learn. Like being sneaky. You've shown me how useful it is. Even a short trip. I'm a fast learner –."

"No," Echo said flatly. "There are strict rules about this, and for good reason."

"Alright; forget I asked." Even to himself, Pastel sounded petulant. But not wanting to be alone he asked, more to keep the conversation going than out of genuine interest, "So what's this project of yours?"

"It's quite an honor, really." Echo replaced the image in front of them with one of an 'older neighborhood'-style galaxy, highlighting a particularly dense region. "See this area? It's becoming way too full. So many stars so close together are causing increasingly erratic orbits among those few planets on the outskirts which could still support life."

Even to Pastel's inexperienced scrutiny it seemed impossibly crowded.

"I've managed to get on the team researching the best place to create what humans call a 'black hole'. Know much about that process?"

"Not really," Pastel admitted. He'd always contented himself with using the time-space amenities others put together.

"It is extremely useful as a recycle mechanism. Black holes channel matter into their vortex, crush it down to core fuel and expel it into the opposing universe – matter or antimatter – to eventually explode as a new star. The blast collapses the 'black hole', letting the remaining solar systems return to normal, but with more room to spread out."

"Efficient," Pastel agreed. "But don't you have to make sure there's nothing nearby in the other universe?"

"Of course. That's part of the challenge, finding just *the* perfect spot on both sides. The size of the hole and its intensity are also crucial. You want it to draw only certain items. It mustn't be allowed to pull other bodies so far off course that their intended life cycle is disrupted. I'm strictly a volunteer for now, but . . ."

Pastel stared at Echo in surprise. "You're not quitting the Helpline, are you?"

"Eventually, though I'll probably stay on-call if needed."

Pastel recovered enough to project warmth. "Well, don't be in a hurry to leave."

"The Helpline – no. But the black hole team is gathering. I'd better go before they replace me."

And I'd better find something to occupy myself, Pastel mused as Echo disappeared. *Or I'll go crazy.* He did *not* want another episode like the one that had caught him so off-guard when Whisper and Sirene merged. He was at a crossroads, and for the life of him, Pastel couldn't see any path that didn't lead further into abject loneliness and misery.

Other than working the Helpline, timespacing had been his only passion since leaving his part-time job at the library. While there, Pastel had enjoyed cataloguing and sorting through new ideas and talents explored and contributed by the outfocused. But eventually, the sheer volume and diversity of input had overwhelmed him. Belatedly, Pastel had realized that, instead of just cataloguing the input, he had been trying to assimilate everything new he came across. When Zephyr recommended a hiatus, he'd been quick to agree.

Pastel's mind meandered through the bits of data he had picked up about 'splitting'. Perhaps while learning to do the 'splits', Pastel would discover a useful, or at least entertaining use for his free time.

He was still casting around for something to do when a timid feeling pressed against Pastel's awareness.

Am I intruding? It was Sweet Memory, Team 1's newest recruit.

Not at all, Pastel transmitted, grateful for any diversion. She arrived in a twinkling.

"How did your stint on Team 4 go?" Pastel asked. He knew she had wanted to meet Tower, to reassure herself that he would be alright.

"Okay, I guess. Tower is putting up a brave front, but he seemed distracted."

"I expect he will be for a while." Pastel noted the discomfiture Memory was trying to hide, and suspected it had nothing to do with Tower. "Is there something else on your mind?"

"Well, yes, sort of . . . It's just that I feel like people are shunting all the easy calls to me. As if they're afraid I'll botch it if I get a tough question."

Pastel imaged a slow nod. "They are. And I am, too, when we're on shift together. But not for the reason you think."

"What other reason could there be?" Memory's output dimmed in distress.

Pastel unobtrusively leaked as much reassurance in her direction as he dared. If he didn't handle this just right, he was pretty sure she would bolt. "We're not afraid you'll frighten the callers away," he told her gently. "We're afraid you'll frighten *yourself* away, if you feel you messed up."

"Oh." Memory was silent for a time. "Then you think I'm too timid for the job?"

"Personally, no. But you're the only one who can decide that. It's can be tricky, when timespacers ask you for input in their lives. They take it all so seriously. It's easy to get intimidated, to think you could ruin their whole trip with one careless comment or poor choice of words. Or that they might misinterpret or misuse what you say."

"Exactly. That's *exactly* what I'm afraid of."

Pastel nodded, remembering his early days on the job. "That's in part why we handle the Helpline as a team. If one of us runs into trouble or says the wrong thing – and we all do (some more than others)," he admitted candidly. "Another can step in and reword it before the timespacer gets the wrong idea. That's also why we speak with the same 'voice', more or less. Most times, humans don't even realize they're speaking to different entities when they call in, even with us using the term 'we' a lot."

"That's a relief. I was wondering if I'd made a mistake by joining the Helpline." Memory's emanations regained a healthier glow.

Pastel projected warmth and approval. "You're doing just fine, and we're really glad to have you."

There was a pause before Memory said, "It probably wouldn't hurt either if I got in a few more time-space trips. I've only had three, you know, and I didn't do anything very challenging. It would probably make me a better Helpliner, wouldn't it?"

"Most likely. There's nothing like experience to fill in the blanks. Say, I've an idea." Pastel felt a rush of wild hope collide with shock at what he was about to suggest. "Why don't I accompany you, in whatever capacity you wish?"

"Oh, Pastel, would you?"

Memory's gratitude made Pastel feel like a psychic cesspool. *No – just say 'no',* he ordered himself.

"It would be my pleasure," he heard himself say instead. "And since I'll be sort of mentoring you 'in the field' . . ."

As he had hoped, Memory cut him off to say, "Of course! It's only fair. Use one of my trips; I've got more than I'll ever need."

"Then it's settled. But let's keep it to ourselves until just before we leave, alright?"

"Sure, if you really want to," Memory said with evident reluctance.

Pastel had a sudden, overwhelming desire to escape Memory's scrutiny. "We'll talk about it later, alright? I've got to go now." Before she could reply, Pastel threw himself into the first vacant patch of nonspace he could find.

And there he crouched, shaking with reaction, revolted and appalled by what he had just done. How could he sink so low? He'd overheard a snatch of conversation recently, a rumor that he was a time-space addict. Could it be true? Pastel whimpered deep within his being as an even worse possibility hit him: What if Memory told Murmur about his deception? He couldn't bare the thought of Murmur hating him, seeing him for the fetid loser he must be, to pull such a heinous trick on a sweet 'kid' like Memory.

There was only one solution. He had to call it off, right now, and hope against hope Memory never breathed a word of it to a living soul. But when Pastel checked, Memory had already hooked up with a friend. He dared not intrude lest he raise her suspicions further. But would she keep her promise until he could get her alone and cancel the arrangement? The more he thought about it, the less likely it seemed.

Finally, unable to bear his thoughts a moment longer, Pastel presented himself to Fjord, Team 2's elder, and volunteered for the upcoming shift. He had never met those Helpliners and, with any luck, word of his problem would not have reached them yet.

*

"Offworlders are coming."

Pastel could hear the desperation in Clarity, aka Aria's voice. Her precognitive abilities had grown strong of late, as had her ability to reach the Helpline 'on the fly'. Right now, she was sprinting toward what passed for the defense headquarters of the human colony on Shawnika.

"I *knew* we'd be attacked if the Orions learned we were here. I warned our leaders against this planet," she told Pastel, panting as she ran. "But they wouldn't listen. The fools even dismantled our ships to build houses. Now we'll all be killed."

Of course, that was part of the 'script' Clarity had approved before assuming the persona of a 23rd-century seer. Pastel knew that the colony and all its inhabitants would be destroyed, as Aria had foreseen.

Before the excursion began, each colonial focus had agreed to exit the game at that point. Part of the challenge was to complete as much of their primary goal as possible before the termination event. As always, a few enterprising souls had signed on sight unseen. They would use the added challenge of an unanticipated environment and unknown exit point to further test their burgeoning skills. And of course, the group included many who sought only the infantile or in-utero experience.

Now it was about to end. Pastel found mass departures the most trying, for usually his job was to assist timespacers. In this case, he not only had to remain idle, he could not even confirm Aria's prediction.

"You have done your best." Pastel assured her lamely.

"Is there any way out of this for us?"

Pastel hesitated. He would not – could not – lie, but neither could he say anything which might change the timeline. Only timespacers had the right to modify their travel itinerary. "We are not permitted to interfere with your life pattern," was all Pastel could say.

"I know. But surely a suggestion or two wouldn't hurt. Or . . . wait! Is this a cusp?" Aria asked, with sudden insight.

"Yes." Leaving time-space definitely constituted a cusp.

Aria reached the shelter and came to an abrupt halt just outside the door. "Then maybe there *is* something I can do!" And with that, she terminated mental contact.

"Oh-oh." Pastel turned toward Fjord. "Have you been monitoring?"

Fjord produced a fine rendition of a snort. "2,583 outfocused involved – and I wouldn't be listening?"

"Okay; silly question. Thing is, Aria's resourceful and talented enough to affect the outcome. I know we can't veto her choices or sabotage her efforts –"

"No, we can't."

"– but we'll have a lot of disgruntled folks to answer to if she postpones their exit."

Fjord shrugged. "It wouldn't be the first time. Don't forget, they are *always* changing their minds, rewriting their lives to greater or lesser degrees. If it was all preplanned, there wouldn't be much point in living it out, would there? They go in knowing any one of them could revise things at any time. That's part of the fun – not really knowing what's going to happen, no matter how carefully they've orchestrated it."

"So it's alright if Aria saves their mortal butts?" Pastel quipped, relieved to not have compromised all those missions by his less-than-stellar handling of her call.

"In this timeline, certainly. They'll still 'die' in a host of others." The elder gave Pastel a gentle push. "Don't get so caught up in their thinking that you forget how things really work."

If Pastel could have blushed, he would have. "I did, you know. Briefly, but I did."

"I know." Fjord said with quiet severity. "And that is the one thing you must not do."

Fjord's frequency activated and the elder opened to it, flashing Pastel a quick 'smile' of encouragement.

Almost at once, Pastel's attention was attracted by his an incoming call from Bitter Sweet's human extension. "Hi, Danny. Long time since you called."

"Yes. I've been doing okay on my own, and I don't like to be a pest."

Unlike some of our callers, Pastel couldn't help thinking.

"We're always glad to hear from you. How may we help?"

Pastel felt Danny's uncharacteristic hesitation before he said, his voice self-deprecating, "A couple of years back, I watched a documentary on 'end-times' prophecies and had a good laugh. Now we're at war with terrorists who seem to move about at will and may even have suitcase nukes. Those are –"

"Yes, we know what they are," Pastel assured him.

Danny sighed. "Yeah. Anyway, now those prophecies have me worried. The main dates given were the millennium, which we're past, and 2012. I find myself hoping we make it *to* 2012, let alone beyond it. I don't suppose you could tell me how this'll turn out?"

Pastel groaned inwardly. First Aria, whose imminent destruction he couldn't confirm. Now he couldn't tell Danny his civilization would survive their present crisis.

"I'm sorry. All I can say is futures are fluid, dynamic. Prophecies are based on what is perceived to happen, but when people in the foreseen times know of the prophecies, they tend to do a last-minute scramble. Whether or not your civilization survives is in the hands of the people of your time, not ours and not the prophets'."

"But why do we keep doing this to ourselves?" Danny wailed. Pastel could actually hear his teeth grind. "We never seem to learn."

"Yes, you are an 11th-hour species. You love to see how deep in trouble you can get yourselves and still avoid destruction at the last possible moment. It is both a weakness and a strength. Most of you play that game throughout your personal lives, in one way or another. Why does it surprise you that you would do the same as a collective?"

"Good point," Danny admitted ruefully. "Well, thanks anyway for what you *were* able to tell me." With that, he was gone.

Pastel wondered if that last remark had been a subtle rebuke and if he could have handled it better. He was still mulling it over when he heard a gusty shout. It was Open Mind, aka Ricky. In the alcoholic's perception, nearly a week had passed since he had inadvertently picked up on Pastel's thoughts.

"Are ya there? Can ya hear me?" Ricky bellowed in Pastel's mind.

"Loud and clear. Congratulations."

"Took long enough," Ricky grumbled. "I bin tryin' to get ya fer days."

"Now that you have, it'll be a lot easier next time," Pastel assured him. "You seem far more comfortable than when we last spoke."

"Yeah. The D.T.'s have stopped – finally. Got a minute?" Ricky didn't wait for a response before plunging ahead. "Ya know them notes ya had me write down?

Well, I been readin' 'em, and then I got to thinkin', maybe I bin talkin' to the Devil or sumthin'. You ain't the Devil, are ya?"

Pastel sighed. If he had an erg of energy for every time someone asked him that . . . . "No, Ricky, I'm not the 'Devil'. Nor am I 'God' or an angel. I'm your monitor. I'm here to answer your questions if you call, and to offer an overview perspective if you want it."

"What's that?" Ricky asked, his tone suspicious.

"Imagine you were lost in a forest and didn't know how to get out. Now picture an eagle, soaring overhead. The eagle can see you *and* the forest. It could tell you where you are and which routes lead out of the woods, if you could speak to each other. Consider me that eagle, Ricky. I won't tell you what to do or where to go, but I *can* describe what you're doing that you may not realize and list some alternatives. What you do about them is up to you."

There was a short pause. "So yer sayin' you'll help me see, but ya won't help me do, right?"

"Precisely." Pastel projected warm approval. "Is there anything you'd like me to help you see?"

"What am I s'posed to do now?" Ricky asked quietly, all his defenses down. He was 'dry' but still adrift, and he knew it.

Well done, Open Mind, Pastel thought, carefully shielding the sentiment from his timespacing colleague.

"You've already made a good start by deciding what you don't want – the drinking. Now you're understandably afraid to go forward in case you again choose a path you won't like. Yet all your twists and turns have led you to this moment, this cusp. We have a saying here:

Salvation occurs when a miserable person looks at his present and future, and changes his mind.

Your lifetime is all option and no promise. You provide the promises to yourself and fulfill them. I cannot tell you what to do with your life, Ricky; that's your decision. Each decision sets in motion a chain of events. Wise choices offer advantages and opportunities, both recognized and not – the people you meet, the 'doors' that decision will open for you, and so on. When you set goals for yourself and fulfill them, you'll start to feel in charge of your life."

Ricky frowned, considering. "Maybe I could get me a job. I got a buddy; he works in a restaurant, washin' dishes. I can wash dishes."

"It *would* be an option."

Ricky rushed on, gathering steam. "And then maybe I could save enough money to get me an education, maybe even work in a bank or sumpthin'."

"One step at a time," Pastel cautioned. "Always make a goal reachable now, or in bite-sized portions you can grow with. That goes for everything in life. The fastest way to destroy a good idea, direction or decision is to make it too big too fast. People become frightened and discouraged by unrealistic goals and end up shying away from them."

"Then I'll jus' get me a job fer now." There was another pause. "Can I call ya later?"

Pastel projected a smile, knowing his caller would 'feel' it. "Whenever you like."

"Okay. Bye fer now." Ricky's focus disappeared.

"All clear?" Cold Fire asked. A forceful entity with a dense presence, he was manning the next frequency which, at the moment, was idle.

Pastel nodded. "Just finished."

"I've been getting a lot of calls lately from True Colors, aka Aspen. England, circa 1980. I helped her through a messy divorce, but now she's clinging to us the way she clung to her husband. That's something I don't understand, this dependency thing."

His mind awash with recent memories, Pastel said, "I do. I built a whole lifetime around that theme."

"Really?" Fire's gave Pastel his full attention. "I was hoping you had. What causes it, anyway?"

Pastel considered the question. "Let's come at it from the other angle: The thing about independence is that most people fear it. They've been dependent, in one way or another, since conception. They go through life dependent on parents, spouses, friends, jobs, religions or whatever. Real or imagined, those dependencies represent safety and/or security to them. Without that protection – or at least someone to blame if things go wrong – they feel too vulnerable." Pastel paused, vividly reliving the base feeling from that lifetime. "Most people don't want just a safety net or a backup system; they want a shield between themselves and the cutting edge of life. Which means, they seek a more secure and comfortable dependency."

"So how do you wean them of it?"

Pastel reviewed his own gradual withdrawal from dependency during that lifetime, and studiously ignored obvious parallels to his present situation. "Like you would any other addiction: slowly and in stages, and if possible without your callers realizing they are being eased away from the comfort source. Most importantly, at the same time they must develop a new, healthier dependency on themselves. Seed plenty of personal growth experiences which will feel 'safe' to them, to foster self-confidence, but don't rush it. That's what I'd suggest."

Fire waited a pensive moment before he said, "My instructor told us much the same in Basics, but I couldn't get a feel for it.

Maybe I should try living it out, like you did."

Pastel's focus sharpened. "It's always useful. Being omnipotent makes it a hard concept to understand. You might want to add in jealousy and possessiveness; they're also based on insecurity."

"Good idea," Fire agreed. "Might as well do them all at once."

"It won't be an easy lifetime," Pastel warned him.

"No, but I haven't given myself many challenges, the last few times out –." Fire straightened abruptly. "Got to go; caller."

Pastel's own frequency remained silent. He found himself reminiscing about some of the more memorable trips. Each had had its special flavor – some frightening or bitter, others warm and sweet. Each had fleshed out for Pastel some aspect of perception, feeling, creativity, activity or understanding he had previously found hard to grasp. Experience *was* by far the best teacher, and no matter what the rules said, you could never have enough of them. There were some concepts you just couldn't absorb any other way.

A slight tingling alerted Pastel to an incoming call. It was Safe Haven, aka Peter, the 22nd-century Austrian therapist.

"I hope I'm not interrupting," Peter was considerate enough to ask.

"Not at all."

"I've been thinking about maturing, aging and dying. The last two seem to be beyond our control, yet people don't age at the same rate, I've noticed. Is that just genetics or lifestyle, or is something else involved?"

Pastel enjoyed answering Peter's astute questions, and felt himself relaxing as he said, "True-you does not age; you only mature. But your body faithfully reflects how flexible and evolved your timespacial thinking has become. Action-wise, it also reflects your ability to access what you know and act on it.

People tend to bog down ever deeper in mistaken beliefs as they go along. They do this by absorbing new falsehoods and/or reinforcing existing ones. When finally the difference between reality and what they perceive through their biases and beliefs becomes too great, there is nothing left to do but leave. If they wish to succeed in that area, it is much faster and easier to start over than attempt to find the truths behind the billions of lies they believe and cling to so strongly. That is why people 'age' and 'die'."

Peter nodded. "I've dismantled a few of my beliefs, but it sure wasn't easy."

"Perhaps this will help," Pastel said. "Imagine a core belief as a capsule folks swallow. It will usually have a name (say, that of a religion or a sports team). The capsule consists of a set of 'musts' and 'can'ts' which they adhere to, held in place by – what else? Beliefs. In response to the new beliefs, those people will develop a set of responses and behaviors which run automatically from then onward."

Peter wrinkled his nose in distaste, but made no comment.

"Now, about your question: Maturing is learning to tell the difference between what is real and what is not, and to realize that even *that* may change. And, of course, to act accordingly.

As regards the body, remember: What is living cannot die, and what is lent life properties will not lose them – gradually or instantly – as long as the person is living true to himself. The moment his material world becomes more real and valid to him than he does, the bond between the life-giver (his spirit) and the material world (which includes his body) is weakened, and the body starts to deteriorate.

Put another way, the more he focuses on what the world is doing to him instead of on him running his personal world, the less directing and nourishing influence his spirit can have on him. That is because his spirit experiences itself less through him than it experiences his playground."

"Hmm." Peter mused. "So I'm here, but my spirit is – wherever you are?"

"Yes. A small portion of you is a guest there, but only in perception."

Peter unconsciously 'stretched' his focus upward. "So, if I understand you correctly, we can drastically extend our lifetime here by reflecting our true selves. Right?"

"Yes. But be patient with yourself. It takes time to change your mortal body and expectations to immortal perspectives. It starts when you truly accept yourself as a timeless creator, not a time-bound creature. Time was never meant to be your judge, jury and executioner. All time is, is consciousness expressed. It is how humans proceed from one action or perception to the next. But time in itself doesn't exist; you do. Or, to put it another way, this is your life, not your time. You are, period; you are not when."

Peter frowned. "It sure *feels* like time exists. Everywhere I look, I see life begin, age and end."

Pastel could empathize. It was a sticky concept at best. "One of your sister personas devoted much of her life to exploring time. She ran this one by me. See what you think:

Time is a frequency upon which life games are played, just like a radio broadcasts on a given frequency. Each person has her own frequency in both time and space, and decides what she will air (give airtime to) on it. You can tune in to someone else's frequency and listen to him instead of filling your own frequency with what matters to you. But you can't deliberately broadcast on his, nor he on yours.

and this one:

Time releases your thoughts and actions from their simply being, so that you can feel and experience them and measure their value to you."

There was a brief pause, then Peter said, "I've written those down. Do you think she'd mind?"

"You're both the same entity, when you aren't timespacing," Pastel reminded him. "How could you mind?"

Peter chuckled. "Good, then. Thanks, friend." And with that he was gone.

Pastel waited for Fire's caller to disengage. A fierce battle was going on inside of him, and once again he was losing. The instant Fire disconnected, Pastel pounced. "Were you serious about doing a dependency lifetime?"

"Yup. What you said about feelings made me realize I've just been spouting textbook stuff with nothing to back it up. If *I* can't feel it, how can the poor caller?"

"Feelings *are* crucial, if you want them to remember it and take it to heart," Pastel agreed quickly. "Planning to leave any time soon?"

"I haven't decided."

Pastel moved a bit closer and restricted his thought transmission to only Fire. "I wouldn't mind tagging along, you know. There are still some details I need to tidy up."

"Oh? Like what?"

Pastel knew just what those loose ends were, too. "In that lifetime, I clung something fierce. But my lover was reserved. He never really showed what he felt or how it affected him. He just eventually walked away – literally. Went to work one day and never came home. I could go as your mate or offspring, depending on what form you want your possessiveness to take."

"Hmm." Fire symbolically stroked his nonexistent chin. "I haven't even decided on a gender yet. But I wouldn't mind having you along. Maybe you could throw me a few curves-balls while you're at it."

That reminded Pastel. "Well, I *do* need to practice sneakiness. Trouble is, I've used up a lot of lifetimes lately getting valuable experience. Mind spotting me one?" He added, with a casualness he didn't feel.

Fire imaged a shrug. "Sure, why not? I've got plenty."

Inside, Pastel whooped in delight even as his soul gave a sickening lurch. "Then it's a deal."

"I'll let you know when I've got the itinerary worked out," Fire said.

Pastel felt the mental arrival of the last call of the shift. He turned his attention to Aurora, aka Chantal. France, circa 1630.

"*Mon ami,* you must forgive me; I am distraught. You have taught me much these many years and I am grateful. But always there are problems. I get rid of one, and another just like it comes along. *Zut alors,* how many times do I have to get rid of them?" Her mental voice rose in a bellow of frustration.

Normally, Pastel would have taken her rant in stride. This time, it grated on him. Here was an easy lifetime with very few challenges, and Aurora's focus (Chantal) was forever weeping and whining. Not for a minute did she appreciate what a treasure she had – a lifetime.

Pastel noticed that Fjord was watching him closely, for some reason, and quickly muted his annoyance.

"You're attacking the symptoms instead of the cause," Pastel explained as patiently as he could. "That's why they keep coming back. Remember, we talked about that last time? You still haven't done anything about the cause."

Chantal recoiled in surprise. "*I* was supposed to? I thought *you* were fixing it."

As usual, Pastel's advice to Chantal had fallen on deaf ears. "Perhaps this will help. It's something a North American wrote as a reminder to herself. She lived in the 21th century, so a few of the terms may be unfamiliar to you. But I think you'll get the gist of it, anyway:

You are a being who inhabits a body and plays on planets. You direct your body through thoughts, emotions, perceptions and associations you have created between yourself, your environment and other beings. Your body is attuned to your input, both deliberate and inadvertent.

To recognize at any time the areas in which the input from you is seriously flawed, you need only look at the problems it has created in your body, or in experiences between you and others or with your environment.

A problem is not a 'cross to bear'; it is a clue, a gift. Without it, you would remain unaware of the flaw, the virus you've introduced into your personal program. Do not bemoan your problems; decipher what they are trying to tell you. Your problems are 'cheat sheets' for the tests you keep giving yourself. Did you forget to study (yourself)?

Perhaps you long for a holiday from problems. Yet how quickly do you become bored with the 'perfect vacation'? How long could you stand paradise on Earth, with full security and no challenges?

You chose this lifetime because *it is all option and no promises. This is your playground or battlefield of choice – whatever you choose to make of it. It is yours as you have arranged it to serve purposes you have chosen but may not realize.*

Your enemies are not the problems you perceive. Your enemies are the flaws in your thinking, perceptions, emotional attachments and beliefs. Resolve those successfully, and the problems they created to 'clue you in' fall away, having done their job. Happy hunting!"

Pastel gave Chantal a few seconds for that to sink in before adding, "Rather appropriate, don't you think?"

"They do not *feel* like gifts," Chantal sniffed.

"If you could not feel your legs when you were standing too close to the fire, you would not realize there was a problem until you had burned yourself badly. Would you rather have a minor pain and know that something needs your attention, or no pain and be damaged much worse?"

Chantal sighed heavily. "Very well; I will try. *Au revoir, mon ami.*"

"About ready to call it?" Fire asked as Chantal's mindprint faded from Pastel's awareness.

"Yes. Oh, here's my replace-." Pastel halted in dismay. It was Memory, her aura roiling with angry red swatches.

"You tricked me!"

Pastel flushed, casting a furtive glance at Fire. "I can explain, Memory. Let's go somewhere to talk, alright?"

"No!" She gave the impression of stamping a foot. "I told Murmur about our upcoming trip –."

"I asked you not to –." He tugged desperately at her, willing her to relocate anywhere but here.

"– and she said you're a time-space junkie. How *could* you, Pastel?" Memory's essence had turned almost watery, as though she was weeping inside. "I trusted you. I looked up to you. How could you *use* me like that?"

Pastel felt himself shrink into a muddy brown ball of abject shame. "I was just about to go look for you, to call it off."

"Yeah," Cold Fire injected, his voice as frigid as his name. "Because you had just suckered *me* instead. Well, the deal's off, *loser.*" With that, he teleported himself out of view.

For a moment that felt like an eternity to Pastel, Memory faced him, a silent indictment more painful than anything she could have said. All he could do was return the gaze, squirming internally like a frying bug. He couldn't think of a thing to say.

"Get help, Pastel," Memory said at last, disillusionment in every word. And with that she glided away, trailing disgust.

CHAPTER 3

Memory is right; you need help. Are you going? The query appeared in Pastel's awareness without an introduction. None was necessary. Nor did Pastel have to ponder what Whisper meant.

I don't want to seem pushy, Pastel hedged. *Psyches are a busy lot, I'm sure. They've got better things to do than teach a Helpliner to do the splits. Besides –.*

Admit it, Whisper cut him off. *You're terrified. And to be honest, friend, you've a reason to be, the way you've been acting. Get over here.*

If Pastel could have found a hole to crawl into, he would have dove for it. But telepathic as they were 'on demand', there was no place to hide.

He found Whisper loitering near an entrance to the psyche realm. For some reason, its innocuous portal seemed the more intimidating for its drabness. Pastel felt like a psyche might reach out and grab him at any moment. "I've never been in there. Have you?"

"Me? No. But I hear they aren't nearly as pompous as you would expect."

'I hear' usually meant Whisper was making it up. "Who'd you hear it from?" Pastel demanded.

"Doesn't matter." Whisper dismissed the triviality with an imaged flick of a hand. "Anyway, we both know people – friends, even – who've become psyches. You can't tell me they all turned stuffy. Look at Sirene; she'll be one eventually. Can you imagine *Sirene* brushing us off?"

"Not you, anyway."

"Not *anyone*," Whisper insisted. "If you don't believe me, go ahead: look in on her, fast-forwarding to after she's been a psyche for a while. You'll see I'm right."

Pastel gaped at his friend. "Are you kidding me? It's one thing to look in on the outfocused, but Sirene? Here? Not likely!"

"She wouldn't mind. Trust me on that."

Pastel snorted without even trying. "Trust you? That's rich. Especially after the way you –"

Whisper assumed an aggrieved posture. "That wasn't my fault."

"Then whose fault was it? Certainly not mine." It felt good to dish it out for a change, instead of always being on the receiving end. Pastel allowed his public mind to wonder why he even considered Whisper a friend.

"Because I'm the only one you've got!" Whisper retorted hotly. "And that could change, too, *buddy.*"

Before Pastel could retaliate, Sirene appeared and smoothly insinuated herself between them. "Stop it, you two! You're acting like humans."

Pastel moved backwards, his aura flushed with embarrassment. "Sorry. You're right; I can't keep blaming Whisper. What's done is done." Inwardly, he fervently wished he could undo some of his own recent past.

"And just for the record . . ." Sirene pressed her aura against Pastel's while looking pointedly at her mate. "You are *not* Pastel's only friend."

"I know; I was just . . . reacting. Foolishly," Whisper added hastily, when Sirene continued to project a mental glare at him.

Pastel faced her beseechingly. "What can you tell me about psyches? I mean, you're planning to become one, so you must know *something* about them, right? Whisper doesn't."

Sirene looked from one to the other, then settled on Pastel. Her expression radiated exasperation. "You can't be serious. How could you not know? It's all there in the library – what they do, what's necessary to become one – everything. You worked there, Pastel. Didn't you ever check? Wonder, even?"

If Pastel had had feet, he would have shuffled them. "I guess not," he mumbled.

"Anyway, you're about to find out first-hand." Sirene gave Pastel a none-too-gentle push toward the psyche domain portal. "Go. Believe me; you'll feel better afterwards."

"How do you *know*?" To Pastel's dismay, it came out as a wail.

"I just do. Now *GO!*"

"Wish me luck.". Marshaling what little self-respect he had left, Pastel turned to face the threshold. But how would he get in?

Like this, a voice stated, and Pastel was inside.

*

"'Wish me luck'?" the psyche repeated, after Pastel had had a chance to adjust to his surroundings. They were surprisingly similar to Pastel's own realm – beauty where you chose to have it portrayed, and soft, quiet void elsewhere.

"It's just an expression."

"A very *revealing* expression. And a perfect example of why you are here. Time-space illusions have become more real to you than reality."

Though the indictment was delivered with infinite gentleness, Pastel squirmed inside. There was no way he could deny it, and the repercussions were horrible to consider.

"Do not be dismayed," his host said. "It is an occupational hazard. Most Helpliners and 'frequent travelers' fall prey to this type of psychosis eventually, though not often to this degree."

Pastel dared to look up at the massive energy orb. "They do?"

"They do. Each one manifests it in a different form, of course," the psyche continued in a matter-of-fact way. "By imitating the human experience and mannerisms, you and your colleagues now better understand and relate to the outfocused, but it has also accelerated the 'split' in you."

Pastel gawked at the psyche. "Is *that* what you meant by 'splitting'? I thought it was what I did in Streak."

"That, too. But as you could easily have informed your last caller, problems will present themselves with greater magnitude and frequency until you resolve them or they defeat you."

Pastel was sure he saw where this was headed, and the thought of it made him want to retch. His mental voice quaked as he uttered the unthinkable. "You want me to quit the Helpline, don't you?"

"Let us examine what underlies the psychosis," the being said, and Pastel felt sure, by sidestepping the question, the psyche was obliquely agreeing. "You feel most at home in the time-space realm, and the Helpline lets you experience it, however vicariously, does it not?"

Pastel was silent a moment, shocked at how effortlessly this powerhouse had been able to sum up his supposedly private admissions. "I know it doesn't make sense to be omnipotent and feel that way, but –

but I do." Shame smeared itself across his aura in ugly patches of pukey yellows.

"It does make sense when it is the only place you will allow yourself to love."

Pastel groaned inwardly, but the psyche continued, its gentle words tearing at the very fabric of Pastel's being. "In every time-space trip, you explored some aspect of love, yet you sublimate your feelings for one here in your native realm. Why?"

"I don't know," Pastel desperately lied. He felt so utterly exposed, having his innermost feelings paraded in front of him this way, and there was simply no escape.

The psyche extruded a promontory, briefly touching Pastel's aura. To Pastel's immense relief, the feelings of humiliation faded to a mere shadow.

"Better?" the being asked kindly. When Pastel projected a nod, it continued, "You invested much energy and focus at the library, cataloguing – what, near the end? Mostly love. You are drawn to Whisper and Sirene as much because they are pair-bonded as because of your fondness for them individually. Shall I go on?"

Pastel devoutly prayed that it wouldn't, but dared not say so.

"In time-space, you are able to forget your loneliness and for a while savor pale intimacy of body and soul. Love is what you crave above all else – and yet you will not embrace your need. Again I ask, why is that?"

"How can I?" Pastel cried. His essence writhed in pain.

The psyche made no movement this time, but abruptly that sensation eased as well. "We know this is difficult, but it is important that you understand. You cannot leave where you are until you know where you are. And *who* you are. And what you *feel* about who you are. On the Helpline, how do you feel?"

With his emotions muted, Pastel was able to consider the question. "More in control. Definitely."

"And between shifts, drifting around on your own or even with your friends, how do you feel? Think about it carefully."

Pastel didn't have to. "Lonely."

"And?" the psyche prodded.

The silence grew until Pastel could bare it no longer. "Unworthy. Alright, I said it. Are you satisfied?" That was no way to talk to a psyche, but he was beyond caring.

Misery more profound than anything he ever endured engulfed him, yet a moment later that, too, had been reduced to a tolerable level.

"Lonely *because* you feel worthless," the psyche corrected. "And now you know why you have become so dependent on time-space. There you can relieve your emotional isolation, whether or not you feel worthy of love, because you know that, after all, it is only a game. Remember your training:

'You will not allow yourself to have or keep what you do not feel you deserve, nor to leave the denigration you feel you do deserve'.

Fitting, is it not?"

Pastel winced, knowing the psyche was right.

It touched his aura briefly, as though performing a benediction. "And as with everything else, worth is a matter of perspective. Your recent behavior is but a symptom. It was inevitable that you would live down to your low self-esteem, and you will continue to do so until you recognize and accept your true value."

There was a brief pause, as though the psyche expected Pastel to reply. When he didn't, the being said, "We have intervened all that we may. You must make your own choices. Understand, though, that if you do not resolve this, your effectiveness as a Helpliner will also suffer. We would caution you against further timespacing, for whatever portion you would outfocus would most likely defect, diminishing you for all time.

As to your *other* type of 'splits', here is how it is done:"

*

Of course, his friends awaited him on the other side of the portal. The last thing Pastel wanted right then was to bare his soul to anyone else.

Sirene placed herself in front of him, symbolically blocking his way. "How did it go?"

"I learned a lot." Pastel hoped Sirene would let the evasion stand, but of course she didn't.

"You've been analyzed!"

Pastel glided around her. "So what if I have?" It came out a lot more sour than he had intended, but rather than apologize, he just kept going, putting as much distance between him and his 'friends' as he could without actually teleporting.

"Wait up," Whisper called. "I'll catch up with you later, okay, Sirene?"

"Alright." With obvious reluctance, Sirene let them depart.

Whisper would have had to streak to catch up, and to Pastel's annoyance, he did.

"I really want to be alone." Pastel didn't even try to keep the edge out of his mental voice.

His friend radiated sympathy. "That bad, huh?"

"I just need to think, okay?"

"Sure. You know where to find me. A suggestion, though: Think; don't stew."

"Easy for you to say," Pastel muttered as he projected himself to the one garden in all of nonspace. Team 1 had created the colorful floral oasis, and most Helpliners gravitated to it when something troubled them. The blossoms, of course, dispensed calmness and clarity, both of which Pastel needed greatly.

He balanced his essence on a bucket-seated bench amid perpetually-flowering hollyhocks and variegated rose bushes, and considered what the psyche had said. The tacit warning about a segment of his consciousness becoming trapped in the perceptual no-man's-land between time-space and the Native Realm didn't frighten Pastel. In fact, it offered the escape he'd been seeking. All he needed to do was find a way to remove *all* of himself from nonspace. No reprimands, responsibilities, shame and, best of all, no unrequited love he had no right to, despite what the psyche had said. So the only question was, how could he get himself – all of himself – to Earth?

He allowed his mind to relax for a while. Some of his best answers had come to him when he let his imagination roam free. He was just starting to feel a tad better when his thoughts were interrupted by the arrival of a scowling Murmur. She had caught up with him at last, to chew him out about trying to con Memory out of a lifetime.

Without warning, Pastel's self-control snapped like a dry twig underfoot.

"*NOOOO!*" he cried, leaping off the bench to tower above her. "Not another tongue-lashing! Not even from you – *especially* not from you. I've had all I can take. You don't have to tell me I'm a loser and a fool and a useless, pathetic low-life; I already know it. So just go away and leave me alone," Pastel whimpered. He turned away and curled up in a ball.

Murmur watched him uncertainly. "Is that really how you see yourself?"

"Me and everyone else, including you. If I could, you just bet I'd be out of here in a heartbeat."

"You don't mean that." But Murmur's tone belied her words.

Searing-hot anger boiled over in Pastel. He rounded on her, sickly yellow essence swelling like a sun going nova. "Oh, you better believe it! I don't belong here; haven't in eons. You know it and I know it, so don't pretend you're surprised. If I left right now, no one would give a damn, least of all you. So go back to your precious hobbies and – and your studies to become an elder. I want no part of it – or you!"

"You're right about one thing," Murmur said, her 'voice' devoid of all emotion. "You are a fool."

And then she was gone.

Pastel accordioned into himself, his anger spent, sobbing inwardly. He had just alienated the one person for whom he might have stayed. If only he could slip away into the merciful amnesia of time-space and be lost for all time.

*

Murmur caught Zephyr just as he was emerging from quiet contemplation.

"I'm sorry to disturb you," she said. "But I need your help. It's about Pastel."

"Yes, I know. He's reached a cusp – a bad one. But we must not interfere with his choices, no matter how badly we may want to," Zephyr reminded her.

Murmur moved closer to emphasize the urgency. "But, see, that's the trouble: He doesn't think he *has* a choice. I've known Pastel a long time and I'm telling you, he won't stay where he doesn't feel he belongs. And he's just resourceful enough to figure a way out, if he puts enough of his mind to it. I know for a fact he had access to all sorts of high-level information when he was working at the library." Murmur could feel desperation welling up within her. She knew her aura would be showing the telltale emotional imbalance, but at that moment, she didn't care. "You were his instructor, just like you were mine. Surely you can think of some way to reach him? Please try something – *anything,* but please try."

Zephyr was regarding her very closely now. "You obviously care a great deal for him."

Murmur sighed. "I love him dearly. Always have."

"Then why haven't you told Pastel? It could make all the difference."

She grimaced at her elder despairingly. "How could I? He's the most wonderful, unusual, creative person I've ever met, but he's a loose cannon. I keep waiting for him to settle down, and he just gets worse. Right now, if I told him how I feel, he'd glob onto me like the drowning soul he is. I can't let that happen, for both our sakes."

Murmur felt as though she was weeping inside. "Please, Zephyr, I beg you; don't let him self-destruct."

The elder sighed. "I don't know what I can do to stop it. Let me give it some thought."

Murmur bowed her essence in profound gratitude. It was the first time in millennia she had used that gesture.

*

"Do you know why I'm here?" Zephyr asked the psyche who met him just inside the portal.

"Yes. But you know that neither we nor you may intervene further."

Zephyr was careful to keep his references gender-neutral lest the psyche think he, too, was falling prey to time-space psychosis. "Direct intervention, yes. But so far, the being which calls itself Pastel lacks the ability to outfocus on its own. If it is denied access to such knowledge, perhaps eventually it will stabilize."

"No information may be restricted or hidden. Knowledge must be freely available to all," the psyche ruled. "But there may be another way." Momentarily, it deliberated with its peers. Zephyr had only once before been privy to this sort of instantaneous communication, and again it happened so swiftly that he could not identify any individual thoughts. Then he was being addressed again, but this time with a modicum of humor. "In fact, with your 'Pastel', we recommend the opposite approach."

Some time later, a shaken Zephyr returned to his realm. He had been charged with such a risky ploy that he doubted he could pull it off.

*

Pastel was still dispiritedly casting about for a way into time-space when his concentration was punctured by a squeal of delight.

"Pastel?"

The shout seemed to emanate from everywhere at once. Pastel contracted in alarm. How could a caller from within time-space contact him directly – *and* know his pseudonym?

"I'm right, aren't I? You're called Pastel?"

The Helpliner scrambled to hide his confusion. "Well, yes, though we don't actually have names. I just call myself that for fun . . ." But who was speaking?

"I know!" the caller exclaimed. "I *really know!* I feel me, and I also feel you. This is so cool!"

"Felicity?" Pastel made the psychic leap from the precocious child she had been when last they spoke – probably three years ago in her time-sense – to the ultra-self-aware 10-year-old she had become.

"Yup; it's me."

At the speed of thought, Pastel reviewed Felicity's progress since her last contact. Why hadn't Fjord, her primary monitor, told them Felicity was breaking free of her time-space amnesia?

Because she isn't, Fjord transmitted. *Your perceptions have just migrated close enough to time-space for a sharp focus like Felicity to be able to read your thoughts if she chose to* – all *of them.*

"Oh!" Pastel pulled his focus more strongly into the Native Realm, taking care to maintain contact with Felicity.

"Are you upset with me?" Felicity asked, uncertainty coloring her usually-confident voice.

"No, not at all. It's just that most people aren't able to contact us so . . . directly. You have every right to be pleased with yourself. Uh, is there something I can help you with? Or something you'd like to know?" Pastel asked, trying to steer the conversation towards Helpline norms.

"Why are you so unhappy?"

Pastel gasped in horror. Then Zephyr was beside him, corralling Felicity's call. Pastel subsumed his relief, lest Felicity pick up on that, too.

Zephyr tight-banded a single instruction to Pastel: *Stay. But quietly.* That meant emotionally as well, Pastel realized.

"Personal issues," Zephyr replied, speaking as Pastel. "We get those, too, sometimes."

"But you live in Heaven and you're perfect."

"If we were perfect, there'd be no room for improvement, would there? Besides, just like Earth, 'heaven' is what you make it." Zephyr gave Pastel a meaningful glance. "Let me ask you something: If you had all the answers to your important questions, and had done everything you wanted to do with your life, it would be pretty boring, wouldn't it?"

"No, 'cause then I wouldn't have to stay," the child replied with aplomb.

The response blindsided Pastel, and once again he had to scramble to hide his reaction. Felicity was too wise by far for her tender years.

"You never *have* to stay; you do so because you want to, right? And because you never know what might happen next that could be fun or that you'd like to explore?" Zephyr continued, unflustered by Felicity's reply and Pastel's reaction.

"Sure."

Careful to shield his thoughts, Pastel wondered if Zephyr was saying this for Felicity's benefit or his.

"When you leave, do you know what happens to what you acquired?" Zephyr was asking.

Felicity's mind held an image of her doll collection. "Do I get to keep them?"

"Not the toys and such, but the memories and your feelings about them, and what you've learned how to do. That's why it's so important that we stay in touch. We can answer your questions and, through you, sometimes we discover things *we* didn't know. Just like you do on Earth, Felicity, we are always learning new things here and meeting people we haven't met before. Including soulmates."

"Cool." There was a short pause. "Oh! Mama's coming; I gotta go. Bye, Pastel." The link between them vanished.

"Thanks, Zephyr."

The elder projected a smile. "No problem. I was coming to see you anyway."

"Oh-oh." Pastel regarded his instructor warily, but Zephyr appeared not to notice. At the same time, Pastel realized Felicity's contact had done what his colleagues hadn't been able to do; it had helped him achieve a modicum of emotional stability.

"I dug up one of your old exam questions. I'd like you to review it. Hear me out," Zephyr said as Pastel started to object. "It's just a memory-jogger to get you back in learning mode. You've been a senior Helpliner for a long time now. I have an instructor-training program about to start and I'd like you in it. The second session will take place on Earth, in case you're interested."

Whatever Pastel had been about to say vanished. "Earth? We'd be human?"

"That you would. In young attractive bodies, too, I might add. I've cued this to the pertinent part," Zephyr indicated the recorder. "The one where you were asked to respond to a timespacer question taken from our files:

Why must we sleep to re-energize our bodies? And why must we blot out memory of what's going on when we're awake, through sleep?

To apply it to your situation, for 'sleep' think 'return to your native perception'. Of course, the bit about 'body' does not apply, but the rest fits."

Zephyr quickly departed. Pastel looked down at the exam without seeing it. *Earth!* If he agreed to the training, Zephyr would *take* him to Earth. Once there, surely he could find a way to escape.

He was so excited by the unexpected boon that Pastel almost missed Sirene's exultant whoop, *"Eureka!"*.

*

"Look!" Sirene projected a thin silvery thread of focus along the seamless conjoint of the matter and antimatter universes her team had finished pairing up. "You can hardly see where we merged them." Sirene was positively quivering with excitement.

Pastel switched his perspective to a vast overview, to better witness the sparkling, elaborate ecosystem spinning in the non-polar plasma of space. Now the Solar System and Spacial Phenomena Specialists could take over, introducing elements which, over time, would produce a paired universe full of objects and options with which timespacers could interact.

"It's exquisite," Pastel said. "How did you get it so precise?"

Sirene conjured up an eye-roll. "You wouldn't *believe* how tricky it was. We had to make sure every single dot of each universe along that line touched its sister point with just the right force. There's not a ripple or a bunch anywhere!"

Sirene glowed with such brilliance Pastel inadvertently leaned back. "It's remarkable. Congratulations."

"Thanks." Sirene's smile widened and she summarily forgot Pastel's existence as her mate arrived.

"Sorry, love," Whisper rubbed Sirene's aura. "I couldn't stop what I was doing just then. But I'm all yours now." He flashed a humorous grin at Pastel before being engulfed in their physical and emotional union.

This time, Pastel found himself unable to enjoy their reflected bliss. In fact, if he wasn't mistaken, what he was feeling was jealousy. His only two friends, and he begrudged them their happiness. Just when he thought he could sink no lower, he had found a way.

Disgusted with himself, Pastel relocated to an empty portion of nonspace. The sooner he removed himself from this place, the better it would be for everyone. But to do that, he had to take Zephyr's courses, the precursor being a review of his old exam.

Pastel reread the question (Why must we sleep to re-energize our bodies? And why must we blot out memory of what's going on when we're awake, through sleep?), before turning his attention to the answer he had given so long ago:

Keeping your mind unaware of your spirit (which are one and the same) requires a split in concentration. It is like trying to make your body do something without letting your mind know about it: It takes your mind to think up the idea, make the decision and tell the body what to do. Then you make yourself forget having done so, and experience the body taking that action 'on its own'. Keeping your two focuses separate and unmindful of each other uses up a great deal of energy.

A spirit like you might use time-space excursions to explore:
- the consequences of living out certain beliefs or perspectives;
- skills development, or re-learning something you already know at your spirit level;
- the 'what-ifs' of having certain events happen to you, or of behaving a certain way. Usually, you'll explore both sides of a behavior or perspective in a single

lifetime, for example, victim and aggressor or selfless and greedy;

- Or, you may use a lifetime as a vacation, to simply have fun.

To make it a fair challenge, you 'forget' that you are running the game. Usually, after many lifetimes, you begin to see 'you and your hand' in every game you play. That is when you truly recognize it as a game – real in substance, but not in essence. The experience and understanding you come away with is the essence.

Long-winded, wasn't I?, Pastel thought. *No wonder Zephyr kept stressing brevity. Those reminders must have been directed at me and I was too egotistical to notice.*

If you did not regularly sleep or 'tune out' your time-space, you would have no opportunity to regroup and start fresh. 'Time out' lets you awaken with a different point of view, free of earlier reactions to recent events. It gives you a fighting chance to succeed, and keeps you from running down too badly, energy-wise.

The more you are being your true (native) self, the less drained you will be at the end of the day. A 'true-selfer' is always at his most comfortable energy level and doesn't require sleep. Like food, temperature control and other human 'needs', sleep becomes strictly optional.

Life needs no support. It is constant and indestructible. When you (as spirit) are feeding life properties to your body, and timespacing-you are conducting it purely and without restrictions, your body also becomes a pure energy expression. That is the only point at which, as a timespacer, you can truly call yourself a 'living' human being.

Pastel turned off the recorder. What had happened to the passionate, confident soul embarking on an exciting new career? What had caused him to plummet so low? *The specter of eternity without love, that's what*, he thought grimly. No place was home without love, and a one-sided love was worse than none at all. It was an immortal wound that would fester and grow till it consumed him entirely.

Murmur had a wonderful future here, one which didn't include him. If he stayed, his love for her would eventually leak out and might undermine that future. No, Pastel decided solemnly, the only way to protect her and be a true friend was to leave and never return.

Martyrdom, he soon discovered, felt infinitely better than self-loathing. Pastel shamelessly wallowed in it, soaking up its soothing saintly undertones, until Zephyr called him to class.

CHAPTER 4

When Pastel arrived, he was surprised to find only two other graduates seated in front of Zephyr. As usual, his instructor did not bother with small talk.

"Pastel, this is . . .". A feelingful image of tingling crystal flame identified the selfhood to one side, as Pastel approached the one vacant chair between the two. ". . . who is calling himself Solar Flare for the purposes of our verbalized expression. He has worked exclusively with Orions."

"Our target species interfaced briefly," Flare noted, by way of acknowledgement.

"Through a human called Aria on Shawnika," Pastel supplied.

Flare bowed his upper extension. "The Orions call that planet Shusqi. It will be interesting to see how my caller, Bruth, the captain of the lead ship, modifies her mission. Like you, I may not preview the balance of her lifetime, now that she has pivotally changed it."

So Aria found a way after all, Pastel thought. The knowledge heartened him, both for her sake and his. If Aria could change her entire planet's destiny, then maybe Pastel could change his own as well.

"What caused Bruth to decide against destroying the colony?" he asked.

Flare radiated quiet amusement. "Aria mentally reached her. Somehow, Aria managed to convey the fact that she also talks with us here. According to Bruth, Aria described in graphic detail through imagery what Bruth's forces planned to do to her colony, ending with the single question, 'Why?'. How she could get an intangible like 'why' across the language barrier is puzzling. But Bruth decided that any species advanced enough to contact our realm *and* her must not be destroyed." Flare's aura rippled enigmatically. "The other outfocused on Shusqi might not thank Aria for that intervention, when they finish their extended lifetimes."

"Indeed," Zephyr agreed. "Unless the changes make it worth their while to remain."

Flare projected a nod. "If Bruth can forge a psychic link back to Aria – which she was planning to attempt – it could create some interesting permutations." Now he turned to his companion, who was waiting patiently to be introduced. "This is . . .". Her presence came across as spiced fluidity. ". . . my instructor. She wishes to be known here as Nebula. Besides Orions, she also answers Sagittarian calls."

"Wow!" Pastel exclaimed. "I've heard they use circular reasoning."

"That they do. Most refreshing, though like any other stream of logic, it has its drawbacks," Nebula said.

"If you're already an instructor . . ." Pastel left the sentence unfinished, his query directed as much at his own teacher as at Nebula.

Zephyr motioned them to be seated. "Nebula is here at my request. You have only been exposed to lineal humanoid thought patterns, and Nebula and Flare have had no direct training re humans, although both have time-spaced as one a few times. A bit of cross-training will benefit all of you."

Pastel found himself wondering what it would have been like to timespace as an Orion or Sagittarian. In all the trips he took, never once had he considered being anything but human. It made him realize how much he might have missed.

"We will begin with a caller question and an event," Zephyr was saying. "You will be mentally blocked from each other, to let you record your response without distraction. It is from a distraught survivor of a vehicular collision which, from his perspective, took the life of his only child." Zephyr activated the recording, and the father's voice, choked with unbearable torment, filled the room.

Why did my daughter have to die? *WHY?* It should have been me. She had her whole life ahead of her.

"Do not rush this," Zephyr said. "And remember, you are addressing that grieving father, not me. It is *he* who you need to help, *he* who needs to understand." With that, he turned away.

Pastel mentally replayed the anguished appeal of a father overwhelmed by the unthinkable. Pastel's compassion went out to the anonymous man. From personal experience, he knew only too well how thoroughly a sudden loss could stop a person in his tracks and crush his will to live.

Pastel moved to engage the recorder, then hesitated. Words might explain the 'why's, but what cold comfort they would be! Only one thing Pastel could think of would ease the pain: contact.

"I will let you chat with her now. Do not be surprised if she seems different. She is still the loving person you knew, but she is so much more. Stand by. [At this point, I would let them talk, so the father could experience her continuity and achieve closure for himself.]"

Pastel turned off the recorder and waited for Flare and Nebula to finish. The Orion instructor was speaking quickly, her student a bit less so. That was all Pastel could discern with Zephyr's damper in place.

While he waited, he realized how good it felt to be a student again, and to be responsible for only one question or topic at a time. No one here was angry at him. Best of all, there was no guilt to contend with.

Presently, Nebula finished, and Flare turned off his recorder shortly afterwards. Zephyr removed the barrier between their minds.

"What approach did you use?" he asked Nebula.

"A logical, informative one. The caller is drowning in his emotions. I used objectivity to help balance that." Nebula cued the recorder.

Life exists, no matter what you do with it, no matter how hard you may try to throw it away. Life is, and anything which has consciousness and is life always remains that way. In a time-space, what you see as being alive isn't really. It has merely been lent that realm's version of life properties. But it does not truly experience what it is to be life and consciousness; it can only experience a pale approximation which humans call being alive and conscious.

Put another way, by focusing as a limited-life-expressing and limited-focus identity, the timespacing spirit (you) more closely experiences being 'dead' than you could ever experience it in your native state.

That doesn't mean you long to disconnect from your game. After all, you in part created that playground to let yourself explore problems and experiences of your choosing. To truly enjoy a game, you must be immersed in it.

When a 'family' is experiencing a time-space lifetime together, they each have their own purpose for being part of that family unit, and they each have their own point of departure from that association. The various members may decide to use an 'accident' as a means of going their separate ways or to trigger a major change in attitude or direction. One or more of them may have finished exploring their time-space experience all they wish to or have finished their goals for that excursion. They may use the 'accident' to sever the focus. At the spirit level, all participants know what each will be using the pivotal event for. It is not an 'accident' at all, but a joint decision being carried out.

The most difficult part, for those remaining in time-space, is that they can't remember, as they do at the spirit level, that each family member *did* decide to do this, and for what reason. It is this lack of understanding which often prevents those remaining from resolving their profound sense of loss and accepting the changes the event has brought about in their life.

To be able to think from the spirit level (or at least, to obtain overview perspectives from that level) is to understand the 'why's and that there are no 'accidents'. It is the first step toward having no regrets.

Zephyr turned to Pastel. "Opinion? And reason for that opinion."

Pastel didn't quite know what to say. The answer was indisputably accurate, and had the caller been further along in his emotional recovery, it might have been just what he needed to hear. But right then, with it so fresh and raw . . .

Pastel gave Nebula an apologetic look. "Forgive me, but your response seems, well, *cold*. Like it doesn't matter to you personally how badly he's hurting, or how disoriented and adrift he is."

Nebula shrugged it off. "He would have to face it sooner or later. Better to do it now and save himself the discomfort. He's already hurting all he can; I felt he would barely notice the extra now. Pull the bandage off fast, rather than slowly."

"Be careful with grief and desperation," Zephyr cautioned. "The will to continue can become very tenuous."

"Orions and Sagittarians perceive death very differently from humans. Perhaps I have not taken into account human emotional frailty," Nebula admitted. "It has been a while since I timespaced as one."

Zephyr nodded, then turned towards Flare. "And your approach?"

"I revised my answer partway through."

"Yes, I noticed that."

Flare started to image a diagonal head-movement, caught himself and changed it to a nod. "I did a brief stint as a human lately – just till puberty – and recalled how strongly they believe in their emotions. Here's what I changed it to:

Your daughter had to return home because a project she wanted to be part of was about to begin. Although you do not remember it, you both agreed to this arrangement. You are colleagues here and have timespaced together on numerous occasions. Be assured she is happy and in perfect health. She looks forward to showing

you her newest achievements when you return, many decades from now in your time-sense.

Both Nebula and Pastel agreed that such a response would likely ease the father's mind, if not assuage his loneliness.

Then it was Pastel's turn. He replayed the brief introduction of a mental reunion between the caller and his 'daughter', then waited for the others to react. He knew it shouldn't make any difference to him what they thought of it, but for some reason it did.

"Wouldn't he become dependent on speaking to his 'daughter' whenever he could?" Nebula asked.

Zephyr said, "Surprisingly enough, no, though it does happen occasionally. We've found most callers just ask to speak with their 'departed' once or twice more, and then leave it at that. It's just reassurance they're after, that their loved-one is well and happy."

"How did the original Helpliner handle it?" Flare asked.

Zephyr didn't glance at the 'file' beside him before replying, "The call was shunted to the team elder. She mentally coached the returned focus, who was not a Helpliner, by the way. The 'daughter' consoled the timespacer and educated him on the mechanics of time-space trip purposes, 'accidents' and exits, then animatedly described her native career and hobbies. The 'daughter' also referred to her true relationship to the caller and one of the pursuits the caller's own native self was involved in. The resulting sense of continuity made all the difference for the caller. Afterwards, he was able to get on with his 'life', far less weighed down by the loss."

"Useful," Nebula admitted. "I will remember that."

Pastel made a mental note to do so as well – not that he would be on the Helpline much longer, he reminded himself. That would be the one thing he would miss. Well, that and Whisper and Sirene and Streak. And most of all, Murmur.

Before those thoughts could depress Pastel, Zephyr tapped a psychic file which lay beside him.

"For your second task, you won't be simulating verbal contact. Your job is to prepare a small intervention on behalf of a timespacer at a cusp. Here's the situation." This time Zephyr briefly consulted the file. "Sandy is a young woman who is always afraid that something bad will happen to her. She expects it emotionally as well as mentally, and so has been drawing a series of increasingly dangerous 'near misses'. She is not a caller, so we don't have that 'in', but she lives alone and often slips into reverie. There she experiences the visuals without directing them. That is how you will assist her – by inserting imagery."

Pastel smiled. He could already imagine a variety of ways he could get the message across. But one detail was missing. "What are we trying to tell her?"

"That's up to you. I have described the problem. You find a viable solution and an appropriate delivery method." As before, Zephyr turned away, implying they were on their own.

So . . . how to convince Sandy she's safe. Spontaneously, Pastel felt his own mind sliding into reverie, the home of imagination and 'dry runs'. He watched as images and snippets of memory paraded by, sorting through possible solutions until one 'sucked him in', feelings-wise. If it did that to him, chances were good it would hit home with Sandy as well.

When he looked up, he saw Nebula leaning back, looking satisfied. Flare was radiating smugness. That was when Pastel realized how long he had been in reverie. He looked an apology at his instructor.

"We'll start with you this time, Pastel," Zephyr said at once. "Your solution?"

"I inserted a visual of her sitting in a rocking chair at the edge of a cliff, with a free-fall of thousands of feet if she went over the edge." Pastel paused for effect.

Nebula looked distinctly surprised and Flare's mental eyes narrowed, but Zephyr refused to rise to the bait.

"Then I had her see herself as a fluffy white kitten clinging to the shoulder of a strong person who was trying to comfort her. The kitten's eyes were glassy, her mind focused on that perceived danger. The kitten was unaware that she was safe. She did not notice the comfort and security she was experiencing at that moment in the person's arms, only the illusion her mind was mired in. The person holding her was supremely in control, but unable to get through to the preoccupied kitten. What do you think?" Pastel looked at his colleagues before settling his focus on Zephyr.

Nebula projected a frown. "How certain are you that Sandy could infer her own safety from that vision?"

"I did it with feelings, letting her experience the kitten's perception and, following that, the situation as seen from the eyes and feelings of the person holding her. Here – I'll show you." Pastel opened his mind to them, running the scenario like a movie.

Nebula bowed her upper extremity marginally toward Pastel. "I withdraw my objection."

"Should work," Flare agreed.

"Satisfactory," Zephyr stated. "Flare?"

The Orion Helpliner glanced at Nebula before saying, "I took a different approach. I had her confront her worst fears and battle them in the form of imagined foes. In the story, she was outraged that anyone would dare to attack her, and used that anger to wreak havoc on them. They turned tail and ran, trailing blood from their noses and holding their crotches. It ends with her slamming the door behind them with a satisfying thud. The way I figured it, replace one strong emotion with another more positive one."

Pastel grinned. "Works for me." The course seemed to be helping his own self-image, too, he realized, although he still quite fancied himself as a martyr, bearing his 'cross' in silence.

"Nebula, what's your solution?" Zephyr prompted.

"I portrayed her as a healthy senior at her 80th birthday celebration. I showed her surrounded by her children, grandchildren and great-grandchildren, a loving husband, big cake and a mountain of gifts. I let her feel her sense of security, her pride in herself and her large family, and her deep satisfaction with her life."

"Wish I'd thought of that," Pastel remarked. How better to reassure someone they'll come through it safely than in retrospect?

"An elegant solution," Zephyr agreed. "As both Nebula and Flare demonstrated, when a timespacer is using emotions and beliefs against herself, one valid approach is to 'fight fire with fire'. Negate her fears by making the feelings attached to your inserted event more real to her than the ones she has been experiencing."

Pastel could think of a dozen ways easy to use that sort of approach.

Zephyr rose. "Thank you. That's it for the refresher. Now that we know we work harmoniously together, in spite of the different species we assist, I'll set up the first of your instructor courses. As I told Pastel, it will take place on Earth in human bodies."

Home. Pastel smiled inwardly. He was about to become the first person ever to remove his entire being from reality.

*

Whisper and Sirene were occupied, so Pastel returned to the garden. Now that the decision was made, he felt a serenity which had little to do with the flowers' calming emanations. Hadn't he experienced the same sensation during the lifetime he ended by suicide? That inner peace, clarity of purpose? Once it returned home, the timespacing part of him had regretted its early withdrawal from the game.

But leaving reality was the only true form of suicide. Would Pastel again regret his choice, after it was too late?

An internal 'burp' alerted him to the start of his regular shift and, glad to escape the 'second thoughts' he had been having, Pastel relocated to the Helpline.

CHAPTER 5

"– and they never came." Clarity, aka the Shawnikan colonist Aria, reported perplexedly, albeit with great relief. "The alien merchants who trade with us say that Orions can never be deterred once they've chosen a target. But their strike force should have been here a week ago. I mean, I'm ever so grateful, but . . . You didn't help us after all, did you?"

"No. It is not permitted," Pastel told her, still feeling guilty on that score.

"Well, someone must have. I tried to reach them mentally, like I do with you, but –. Say, you don't suppose it worked?"

Pastel weighed the wisdom of replying, then took a chance. "If someone *did* get your message, it might have made a difference. In fact, that person could be trying to contact *you*. Now, I'm not saying someone *is*", Pastel hedged, mentally glancing at Zephyr, who was closely monitoring the conversation. "But just in case, you might keep a telepathic ear peeled."

Aria grinned. "Make sure they don't get a busy signal?"

"Something like that."

As Aria's focus departed, Pastel turned towards Zephyr. "Acceptable, under the 'occasional directing' clause?"

Zephyr imaged a waffling hand. "It was borderline. And *only* because her message was received by a fellow caller."

"Understood." Pastel relaxed a little.

A familiar niggling sensation heralded the next incoming call. It was Twisted Humor, aka Gail. A quick mental check confirmed she hadn't been in touch for nearly a month (her time-sense), which was highly unusual.

"Hello, Gail. How may we help you?"

"I know I've asked you this before, but I just can't seem to get a handle on it. I have nothing to feel vulnerable about, but I still do. How can I develop a sense of confidence and security?"

"Actually, those are quite different," Pastel explained. "Confidence is knowing what you can do. Security comes when that confidence is deeply felt and unshakable. Confidence can be generated, instilled, increased; security cannot. If a person is not secure in herself, no amount of support or protection will produce it, because security comes from within. It cannot be generated from outside."

"Then how can I develop it?"

Pastel hesitated. Recently, Echo had played hardball with her, and it had worked. Perhaps it would work again, if used judiciously. "A good start is to look at what base you are building your future on. Skills and goals? Purposes? Feelings of kinship with what you desire and therefore pull from your environment? Improved standards of living? Better decisions? Or history lessons? Do you use yesteryears to identify the mistakes you'll never make again or to relive past traumas? What are you projecting into your future, based on your thoughts, beliefs and emotions or feelings? And from the answers to these questions, what would you expect your future to be?"

"Trouble," Gail admitted. Pastel could feel the shudder that ran through her body as she realized the implications. "No wonder I feel insecure."

He steeled himself to punch through. "Don't be afraid of your thoughts and feelings; take *responsibility* for them. For they (which means you) are responsible for your future. You are giving yourself good reason to feel insecure, because you are seeding the worry-filled events that befall you."

Gail was silent for a few moments. "I hope I can reverse them." Her tension was almost palpable.

"You can; of that we are certain." Pastel stopped short of telling her that she would. That future was for her to decide and create, not him.

"Thanks."

With the frequency clear again, Pastel projected a cocked eyebrow, and Zephyr nodded. "It was within parameters. Use it sparingly, though."

"I will." Pastel previewed the next year-and-a-half of Gail's life, carefully seeding experiential options which, if she made use of them, would help her overcome at least some of her insecurities. When he returned his focus to the Helpline, Pastel noticed that all frequencies were idle.

Mind if I listen in on your calls when I haven't any of my own? Zephyr is training me as an instructor, Pastel transmitted to his teammates. Even the innocuous request gave him a pang of guilt. Pastel deeply respected Zephyr, yet he had no intention of using the course for any purpose other than to serve his own selfish need. Or was it selfless, removing himself to where he couldn't interfere with anyone else's (such as Murmur's) career path?

There was a flurry of activity on the Helpline. Of the four replies (including Zephyr's), three overlapped. Pastel had to scramble to confirm he had received unanimous consent to listen in. It would be useful, he assured himself, to see how the other Helpliners handled questions. As one of the tenets of reality stated, there is never only one way. He owed it to Zephyr to at least do his best in the one course he would take.

When Sweet Memory nodded toward Pastel, indicating someone was coming on-line, Pastel mentally screened out all input, other than monitoring his own frequency and Memory's.

"Hello, again," a mental voice Pastel recognized as belonging to Wise Acre, aka Cindy the sage, said brightly. "I've got a few more aphorisms, if you'd like to hear them."

"We always appreciate your thoughts." Memory leaned forward eagerly to capture them on her psychic recorder as Cindy began her recitation. Pastel couldn't record someone else's telepathic contact, so he made notes instead. He always enjoyed adding her maxims to his collection. That was another thing he would miss when he permanently withdrew.

Memory waited long enough to be certain Cindy had finished reading them off before saying, "Those are excellent observations. Do you keep a spare copy of them someplace secure?"

Cindy patted her sheaf of papers. "That I do."

"Good. We have a few you might enjoy as well."

"Okay, I'm ready."

Pastel felt Memory's mind switch to retrieval mode. Most of the ones she gave Cindy were known to Pastel, but a few weren't, and he added those to his list as well.

"May I use some of these with my clients?" Cindy asked.

"Certainly. Although we would not recommend that you divulge your source or disclose those sayings which deal with your native state."

Cindy snorted. "And get burned as a witch? No, thank you! I am very careful what I say, and I keep my papers well hidden."

"A wise precaution," Memory agreed, and Cindy signed off.

Pastel projected a mental 'thumb's up' to Memory, then turned his attention to Silent Echo. That conversation seemed about to end, so Pastel checked on the only other active frequency – the one monitored by Soft Murmur.

"– remember, you have projected your consciousness and energy into time-space and created a magnificent robot in which to house that projection of yourself to let you experience the 'what happens when's? of your not-yet-understanding'," Murmur was saying.

"I like that," the Austrian therapist, Peter, replied. "Thank you. Now, I have a question for a psyche, if that's possible. Can you put me through?"

"Stand by." Murmur broadcast her caller's request. "Proceed," she told Peter just before a powerful mental presence steered the frequency to itself.

"Can a psyche become human?"

Pastel grinned in delight. *This should be good!* Monitoring psyche input was encouraged, due to its instructional value, but it happened woefully seldom. For some reason, few callers thought to ask.

"The 'I' is a window, looking out from its unchallengeable reality into whatever subset of reality it chooses to create for learning and amusement.

To compact 'I' enough to focus a stream of its consciousness into a time-space is itself a fantastic feat, as is a psyche becoming fully functional in a three-dimensional time-space. The reason is that we have to function on such a small scale accurately, precisely and gently. We have an internal storage of unlimited energy, and consciousness of universal proportions. Moving a ball-bearing would be difficult – not because it is hard to move the ball-bearing, but because it is difficult to move *only* the ball-bearing (and not the planet, say).

Your assumption that a psyche can inhabit a body is inaccurate. A psyche directs a focus, a stream of conscious energy which gives life properties to the body. Conscious energy is a product of psyches, as well as a part of our make-up. But we ourselves as a whole unit cannot fit into a time-space, let alone into a time-space body. There is a limit to how much we can restrict and compact ourselves.

When the timespacing focus is able to merge with that conscious energy stream and draw directly from that source, 'enlightenment' begins to come. And with expanded self-awareness, knowledge and energy comes a memory of skills and of how thought, consciousness and energy affect matter. That is when so-called 'paranormal' – actually, finally normal – skills begin to be used by the timespacer in his world.

Remember, a psyche cannot become human. The human becomes a timespacing psyche. A human psyche occurs from the 'ground up', not the other way around."

"Yipes," Peter exclaimed quietly. He and the Helpliners had felt the psyche's abrupt withdrawal. Having answered the question, it had simply returned the call to Murmur and departed.

"Do you have any further questions?" Murmur was struggling to keep her 'voice' matter-of-fact.

"No, thanks. That gives me *plenty* to think about."

Pastel tried to whistle and failed. "Helpful they may be, but Helpliners they aren't."

"Small-talk is not their forte," Murmur agreed with a smile. "Though that could change . . ." She left the rest unspoken, but Pastel knew she was thinking of how she would respond to callers' questions once she became a psyche.

All lines were again inactive, but Echo made a motion to garner Pastel's attention. "Gail has been trying to teach herself telekinesis. Rather a long-winded name for such a simple process, I've always thought. Anyway, she's doing it all wrong and, of course, getting nowhere. Think I'll give her a little training session in her dreams. Want to watch?"

"Sure." Pastel had never used that technique. "Does it get across? I mean, do they remember afterwards?"

"They do if you insert it near waking and ensure they experience sensations, not just visuals and emotions. I've also found it helpful to run it like a ploddingly-sequential class – no jumping about the way their dreams usually do. Ah!" Echo nodded with satisfaction. "I've found an early weekend morning when she's sleeping in, and she's between dreams. Here we go."

As Pastel watched, splitting his focus between what Echo was doing and Gail's experience of it, the lesson began. An unseen, patient voice was saying, "Watch the pen and feel what I'm doing." 'Offstage', Echo hastily materialized a pen, then switched back to Gail's perception. Slowly, so she would feel the focus involved, Echo moved the pen in one direction, then another, finally raising it to hover effortlessly in place. "Got the feeling? Your turn."

The pen gently returned to the surface of a white, surrealistic tabletop. Gail repeated what she had felt Echo do, but the pen remained motionless. "What am I doing wrong?" she asked.

"You're trying too hard, focusing too deeply. It's a soft, gentle influence, not the override mode you use to physically pick up an object. Do it again, but this time, serenely."

Gail grimaced. She definitely didn't relate to herself as 'serene'. Still, within a few moments, she noticeably relaxed and was able to quiet her mind and emotions to something less forthright. This time, when she applied the technique, the pen moved marginally. A surge of elation backwashed into Echo. Because Pastel was monitoring it, he also felt the wave of delight.

"Good. It's a start," Echo acknowledged the minor achievement. "But keep your emotions and focus steady. You're here to learn, remember. So take it as a 'given' that you'll succeed and that you're just here to practice."

Obediently, Gail struggled to dampen her emotions and bring her focus to bear on the object. This time, the pen moved in various directions before rising unsteadily off the table.

"Stabilize it," Echo instructed. "You want it to be perfectly level and to be locked in at that height."

His student made the modifications, all the while fighting down exultation.

"Now spin it horizontally."

Again, after a few seconds' delay, Gail was able to perform the simple task.

"Good. Now you have the basics. Keep practicing here as long as you wish."

"Will I remember this when I wake up?"

"Yes. The rest is up to you."

A blast of appreciation enveloped the listeners and, of course, the pen fell back to the tabletop.

Leaving Gail to her practicum, Echo withdrew and regarded Pastel. "So, any questions?"

"Did she learn to do it in her waking state?"

"No."

Pastel frowned. "Then why bother giving her the lesson?"

"Options, Pastel," Echo replied crossly. "Remember them? To be offered at every opportunity, or whenever a timespacer puts in effort in a given direction?"

Pastel transmitted a sickly grin. "Oh, yeah. Those."

"*Do* try to keep the basics in mind," Echo said with less asperity.

Pastel looked up to see his replacement standing alongside him. The next shift was arriving.

Zephyr motioned for his team to assemble at the Briefing site, but to Pastel's surprise, once they did, Zephyr remained 'standing'.

"Anything you want to discuss?"

No one spoke, which wasn't surprising since so few calls had been received during the shift.

"In that case," Zephyr said, "Briefing adjourned."

"Murmur, Memory, would you stay behind?" Pastel asked as the group began to disperse. He could see their reluctance, made more evident as they glanced at each other before settling back onto their chairs. "Thanks. I just wanted to apologize, and to let you know that, no matter what happens, I think a great deal of both of you."

"You have a funny way of showing it," Memory muttered.

Pastel sighed. "I know. I just had to think things through. I won't try to borrow lifetimes from anyone ever again. That I promise." He kept his focus on Memory, not daring to look at Murmur.

"Memory, would you excuse us?", Murmur asked pointedly.

Pastel felt himself tense. What was she planning to say that couldn't be said in front of Memory?

"Sure." Promptly, the junior Helpliner disappeared.

"You've made up your mind, haven't you? I can feel it. You intend to leave."

Pastel forced himself to meet her intense gaze. "Yes."

"That's it? Just 'yes?'"

Pastel projected a shrug. "What else is there to say?" He felt oddly distant, as though part of him had already left.

Apparently Murmur noticed the change, for her aura's hue deepened in concern. "What about those of us who care for you? Don't we have a say?"

"You're having it now." The words came out a lot colder than Pastel had intended. "Look, Murmur, you know I've always been a loose cannon. And you were right; I am a fool. But I'm not fool enough to stay where I don't belong. I would never be happy, and I would make the rest of you miserable, too."

He could feel her mind casting around. "There must be a way —"

Pastel touched her gently. "Thank you, but no."

Course is starting, Zephyr insinuated the thought into Pastel's mind.

Be right there. "I'm sorry, Murmur. I have to go now. Thank you for being so kind to me."

She moved as though to stop him. "But – you can't get *all* of yourself out of here, no matter what you do. Surely you realize that."

"I don't have to." Pastel couldn't keep the smugness out of his tone. "Zephyr's taking me."

"He *WHAT?*"

CHAPTER 6

"There you are," Zephyr said, as Pastel arrived beside Flare and Nebula. "We have a lot to cover, so let's begin, shall we?"

Before Pastel could respond, he found himself in a crowded early-21th-century shopping mall. True to his word, Zephyr had given Pastel a fine-looking body. It was male, a Caucasian about six feet tall of slim build with firm 'abs'. He was dressed in black pants and a plain black T-shirt. Further details were supplied when he looked in the mirrored column to his right: 20-some, with longish straight light brown hair and clear blue eyes. Pastel could feel the floor beneath his feet, smell pleasant aromas from the café across the way, hear the hum of people conversing among themselves around the corner from where Pastel and his colleagues stood.

"How real are these bodies?" Pastel asked.

Zephyr reached over and pinched him, hard.

"Ow! Okay, they're real."

Zephyr was slightly taller than Pastel, with a manicured long white beard and a shock of matching wavy white hair. Piercing gray eyes peered out from beneath bushy eyebrows. A gaunt frame and dark blue robe with gold trim completed the probably deliberate impression of a wizard.

Poetic license, Zephyr transmitted, privately confirming Pastel's suspicion.

Flare let out a low whistle, looking around him in amazement. He was clad much like Pastel except his shirt was white, but there the similarities ended. Stocky and a head shorter, Flare had a swarthy complexion, dark eyes and curly black hair. The effect gave him an air of quiet intensity.

Nebula appeared completely at ease with the abrupt embodiment.

"Your instructor training included a trip to Earth, didn't it?" Pastel surmised.

"No, but my lives as Sagittarians taught me to enjoy opportunity when it is presented, and to not waste any of it. I mean no offense." Nebula inclined her head toward Pastel, long brown hair cascading forward as she did so. She was nearly as tall as him, with a flawless feminine shape. Pastel especially liked how her frosty blue outfit set off her generous breasts and hazel eyes.

"None taken," Pastel smiled. "And that's right, you did say you'd time-spaced a few times as a human."

"Ah, there's a bench." Zephyr marched toward it. He motioned for them to be seated, but he remained standing. "Observe the passers-by. I will return." With that, he strolled towards the café.

Pastel and Flare exchanged glances, then looked to Nebula for direction. But she was already people-watching, with an expression of rapt attention adorning her beautiful face. With a shrug, Flare turned his head to the right and followed suit.

Pastel gazed at Zephyr's retreating back. This might be his best chance to escape. There was nothing stopping him from saying he was going to the men's room and just never return. So why wasn't he doing so? They had only just arrived, and it felt too soon, somehow.

Nebula nudged him gently in the ribs. "I suggest you pay attention."

Well, if he wasn't going to leave yet, he might as well do the exercise. Pastel looked around him. At first, it was difficult to concentrate strictly on the passers-by, with so much activity and sensory input vying for his attention. Then a youngster in a throng of shoppers caught Pastel's eye as she tugged at her mother's hand.

"Mommy, Mommy, look!" she begged shrilly. She was pointing a stubby finger at a window display stacked with brightly-colored toys and dolls.

Pastel watched, fascinated, as the girl's mother rolled her eyes. "No, Bess. We have to go home. Come on."

"But Mommy, it's Nikki! The one on TV. . ."

The dance escalated, as Pastel watched. The more the child begged, the angrier the mother became, loudly ordering her to come along quietly. The girl balked, the mother bristled. When that didn't work, she cried, and the mother threatened. The child screamed in tantrum, and the mother bellowed at her.

"Are you observing the crowd?" Nebula murmured in his ear over the din.

He hadn't been, so Pastel switched his attention to the onlookers. Expressions of amusement, contempt, discomfort, anger, sympathy, annoyance and a multitude of other emotions were graphically displayed on various faces. A few were pretending they didn't hear the commotion, nudging their way through the onlookers. Others seemed on the verge of joining the fracas.

At length, the mother glanced up as though just noticing all the attention they had drawn. She picked up the child bodily and rushed her from the mall. As they left, the masks of those who had stopped to watch fell back into place.

No wonder she's an instructor, Pastel thought. He had been watching the 'main event', while Nebula had recognized it as an opportunity to see behind the masks people wore in public.

Pastel spent an interesting half-hour observing each person who came into view.

Finally, Zephyr exited the café, wiping his bearded chin with a napkin.

"I'd give a lot to know where he got the money to treat himself," Pastel told Flare, *soto voce*.

"I'd like to know where he *put* it," Flare said. "Are these bodies *that* functional? I thought they were strictly for show."

"Ah, that hit the spot," Zephyr declared, with every evidence of pleasure.

Pastel had to laugh. "Funny you should say that. Flare was just wondering where you put whatever you had."

"Where do you think?" Zephyr patted his stomach. He looked from Pastel to Flare. "What? You don't think you're worth the real thing?"

Nebula, Pastel noticed, was staying out of it, her expression neutral.

Which brought up an interesting question, which Pastel now voiced. "Just how *did* you produce the 'real thing' without us going through conception, birth and all the rest?" He glanced around to make certain he had not been overheard.

Zephyr shrugged. "There's a lot more to being an instructor than just teaching. Or was that all you wanted to learn?"

"No, but –" Pastel looked at Flare for assistance.

"And whether I do teach you such things depends on how well you learn the early stuff. But for now," Zephyr pointed toward the café with his chin. "If you've done your assignment properly, I might treat you to the excellent coffee they make."

"Coffee, you say?" Nebula arched her fine eyebrows. "What would you like to know?"

For someone who had seldom taken human form, Pastel decided she had feminine mystique down pat. Whenever she moved or spoke, his attention was drawn to her like a magnet.

"Let's find a bit more privacy." Zephyr moved purposefully toward another bench – this one at the far end of the wide corridor. It was flanked on either side by banks and a walk-in clinic, all of which were closed.

If I stay for all the training, I could embody myself any way I want, Pastel thought, realizing the significance of what Zephyr had said. *And no one would be able to drag me back or keep me in nonspace.* He sat down on the bench with the others, trying to hide his delight at the revelation.

Zephyr swiveled his head towards Flare. "What did you notice?"

Flare pursed his lips. "The older the set I watched, the more they hid their true feelings and the less notice they took of others and their surroundings."

Zephyr nodded. "Go on."

"The younger the – let me rephrase that: the younger or *younger-at-heart,* the more likely they were to take time to stare at things they longed for but couldn't buy. They had not yet lost the capacity to dream. Many of those who wouldn't look around them, who just went about their business and got out, no longer embraced the possibility that fine things could somehow, someday be theirs. Of course, others just hate shopping and do a 'dash in, dash out', but that's something different," Flare added.

Zephyr's nodded somberly. "You saw, but more importantly, you *understood.* Good." He turned towards Pastel. "How about you?"

"Thanks to Nebula, I noticed the true feelings of onlookers who were watching a squabble between a mother and her child."

"I saw that 'performance', too. What did you observe?"

"Well, the obvious, of course, about how people in public hide their emotions from others and even suppress them within themselves. But there was something else." Pastel struggled to articulate what he had sensed. "Most of them felt something – either for the child or the mother. I think some perceived the kid as the aggressor, while others blamed the mother. A second group was merely annoyed at the mother for bringing her spoiled brat to the mall." Pastel frowned at his inability to get at the crux of the matter.

"Keep going," Zephyr made a circular motion with his hand.

"People are easily sidetracked?" Pastel knew he was grasping at straws.

"And?"

Pastel grimaced, striving to decipher what it all meant. At length, he let his shoulders sag. "Okay, I give up. What did I miss?"

Their instructor gazed pointedly at Nebula.

She smiled at him, silently accepting his challenge. "Oh, just the pair of pickpockets in league with the mother and child."

Pastel gaped at her. "Are you kidding?"

Nebula shook her head. "I saw her glance at them just as the pickpockets were leaving the scene – pun intended – and she immediately picked up the child and hurried away. Things are not always what they seem," she added mildly.

"And I was watching everyone so carefully. How could I have missed that?" Pastel groaned.

Zephyr shrugged. "It's an occupational hazard. You've been trained to look deep, to see what your callers are missing. But you forgot to pay attention to the obvious."

Pastel shook his head. He'd been caught, fair and square.

"And now, you may all join me for coffee and a sweet." Zephyr headed for the café and commandeered a table for four.

Nebula sighed happily a few minutes later as she inhaled the aroma of the freshly brewed coffee the waitress placed before her. "I'd forgotten how much I like this beverage," she said.

"And how pretty everything is. Well, almost everything." Pastel could just make out the graffiti on the 'No loitering' sign affixed to the bench they had just left. "How long can we remain in these bodies?"

Zephyr waved the concern away with a negligent flick of his fingers. "Since we're

fueling them purely from our essence –
indefinitely. But only part of your tutelage
can be taught here. When we've finished
this part, we'll leave. And I don't need to
remind you that, while we're here, we
must not interfere with anyone else's
timeline." Zephyr gave Nebula a sardonic
half-smile before adding, "But it's okay to
buy a cup of coffee now and again."

"Glad to hear it." Nebula wrapped her
hands lovingly around the cup.

"And I presume that also means we stay
together," Flare said.

Zephyr folded his hands on the table.
"Think of this ecosystem as one big,
multipurpose classroom – which of course
it is, even if most of the timespacers don't
realize it."

"No 'recess', prof?", Pastel wheedled.

"We'll see."

Some time later, Zephyr materialized a
reasonable tip, then got up. His students
filed out behind him. He led them down
the hallway which housed the washrooms,
stopping when they were no longer in
view.

An instant later, Pastel found himself and his colleagues standing on a pristine beach.

"Beautiful as it is, this island is too small and too far from anywhere to be inhabited. This will serve as 'home-away-from-home base'." Zephyr grinned over at Pastel. "So you'll have time for 'recess'."

"In isolation," Pastel tried not to pout.

"Breathtaking isolation, though." Flare picked up a handful of sun-bleached sand, letting the grains trickle through his fingers.

Pastel's eyes took in the palm trees and lush tropical vegetation further inland. Splashes of wild color hinted of flowers and exotic birds. Flare was right; it would be a treat to explore.

Zephyr was on the move again – this time toward a large, flat rock jutting out from the hillside. The rock didn't seem in keeping with the rest of the terrain. Pastel wondered if Zephyr had materialized it – or the whole island, for that matter. They climbed atop the rock, facing the magnificent ocean view.

"Before we get on with your training, I'd like a little feedback. You're all senior

Helpliners. Was there anything in your basic training you *didn't* get taught by your instructor that you now wish you had?" Zephyr leaned his back against an adjacent tree trunk, his body abruptly naked. The others followed Zephyr's lead – Nebula instantaneously, and Flare and Pastel by stripping off their clothes the usual way. Pastel was immediately glad he had, for the gentle breeze felt exquisite on his skin.

"About the training?" Zephyr prompted, when no one spoke up.

Pastel was sitting between Zephyr and Nebula, with Flare in lotus position on the other side of her. Nebula's nubile form distracted him every time she moved.

"Ahem."

"Sorry." Pastel blushed, and forced his mind back to business. Remembering his harrowing experience with Felicity, Pastel said, "I wish I had been forewarned of the risks of perceptually migrating too close to the time-space realm. Oh, and I would have liked more on how to handle callers facing imminent mass exits."

Zephyr nodded. "Noted."

Flare stirred. "We have just the opposite problem with the Orions: There's one faction which venerates male suicide – strictly voluntary, but the younger a person is when he leaves, the more posthumous prestige his family gets. They'd have wiped themselves out long ago if they didn't have such an explosive birthrate."

"So what's your question?" Zephyr frowned. Pastel knew Zephyr didn't specialize in Orion culture, but a problem that rampant had to be addressed.

"How do we get through to them?" Flare was scowling, too, his eyes focused on the horizon, unseeing. "They don't get anywhere near completing the goals they landed with. Then they get home and want to go right back and try again, in the same situation. That cult, I'd guess you'd call it, has a high percentage of telepaths, and many of them 'call home'. But they won't give up their ritual suicides."

Zephyr was quiet for so long that Pastel thought he might have fallen asleep. At length, he said, "They accept the nature of their native realm?"

"Yes, to some extent."

"Have you pointed out that in most instances, martyrs are just masochists with a cause, and that they themselves view their suicide as failure, once they return home?"

Flare sighed heavily. "All the time. Not that it does any good. They flatly refuse to believe it. Most anything else I say they'll accept, but not that. It's been drilled into them since birth."

"How do you deal with it?" Zephyr asked Nebula.

It was Nebula's turn to sigh. "I've used every form of persuasion open to me. Nothing gets through the preconditioning – at least, nothing I've found. They look upon our efforts as a misguided attempt to cheat them of their birthright. They acknowledge that we mean well, so they don't take offense; they just ignore any reference to aborting their upcoming suicide."

"How do they view Orions outside their cult?" Pastel asked.

Flare was watching a beetle scuttle up the rock face beside him. "As lesser beings who cling to a false world. That's part of the problem; they're absolutely right about it being a false world. And true, many 'frequent travelers' are self-aware enough to know when their job is done and it's time to come home." He flopped both hands outwards, palms up, in frustration. "But these guys are making *leaving* the main purpose of the trip."

"I suppose you could have one of the returnees go back as a 'savior-of-sorts', to help them break the pattern." Pastel offered the suggestion reluctantly. Too often, the facts about such individuals were later twisted to serve private agendas. But in a case like this –

Nebula shook her head, eyes troubled. "I don't know which does the most harm, in the long run. The Orions never war among themselves. But if a religion got going there, with the fervor they already have . . ."

"No, I wouldn't recommend it either," Zephyr's voice trailed off, as he focused on some inner train of thought. His students maintained a respectful silence until he spoke again. "They value death. What if you removed the anticipated reward?"

Nebula's shapely lips formed into a smile of understanding. "You mean: 'We must inform you that your departees' constant failure to fulfill their intended goals can no longer be condoned. They are being returned to you *en masse*.'" She arched an eyebrow at Zephyr. "Something like that? Maybe not quite that stuffy?"

"Keep the 'stuffy'. Sometimes a little pomposity helps get the message across."

"This is going to be fun!" Flare rubbed his hands together.

Pastel chuckled malevolently. "And just to make your point, send them all back in the identical embodiment to the one they had."

"Excellent idea," Nebula inclined her head toward Pastel, who flushed, grinning foolishly.

Zephyr leaned closer to Pastel. "Maybe I should have given her a less attractive body. Keep your mind on the lessons."

"Sorry." Pastel was remembering just how beguiling human libido could be.

"Alright, anything else you wish had been covered?"

Flare looked a question at Nebula, who nodded firmly. He turned back to Zephyr. "I think cross-training is badly needed by all Helpliners. More and more people, now, are choosing lifetimes in which their species is meeting and interacting with other sentients. I, for one, am finding it hard to give good counsel."

Nebula placed a hand on Flare's shoulder. "That was why I extended my knowledge to include Sagittarians, now that they know of the Orions. But it's spreading quickly. I hadn't expected Bruth and Aria to forge a contact . . ."

"Yes, our timespacing colleagues are definitely getting more adventurous. I'll arrange an instructors' meeting to set up multi-species training." Zephyr looked at each of them in turn. "Anything else?" When half a minute had passed without comment, he nodded. "Alright, then, enjoy your 'recess' before we get to work."

Zephyr climbed down from the rock, found himself a stretch of soft underbrush and, if the sounds emanating from him could be believed, fell fast asleep. Just in case, Pastel tiptoed away.

Soon he was climbing a narrow animal trail up the hillside. Flare and Nebula were in the lead. Pastel reveled in the feedback his oh-so-human body was transmitting to him. With *all* of him here and able to experience the environment, he finally knew what it could be – was going to be –

like living here permanently. And it was *heaven!* The second thoughts he had harbored melted away, and Pastel knew, without a shadow of a doubt, that this was where he was meant to be. Not on this island, of course, but definitely on Earth.

In the meantime, he would enjoy every moment of his time here while he absorbed the training that would soon let him make this his permanent home. Pastel gazed at the flora around him as he climbed steadily higher. The hill was covered by lush tropical growth, but it was as though he had never really seen it before. With all of him able to look through human eyes, everything seemed much more vibrant, the colors a kaleidoscope of brilliant hues. He reached out to touch leaves, communing with the textures as his fingertips caressed each type of plant he passed. It seemed to take no time at all to reach the summit, yet to Pastel the feast of physical sensations felt like it had lasted an eternity.

Pastel stood there, just drinking in the panoramic view. The vegetation extended downward on all sides. From his vantage point, he could see that the whole island was rimmed by a wide expanse of beach. "Zephyr sure knows how to pick them."

Flare scanned the horizon before him. "You got that right. And no land in sight anywhere. It's a regular paradise."

"Almost makes me want to change career," Nebula said. "Creating beauty like this would be a fine artistic outlet."

"A close friend of mine just seeded germanium-based mobile life forms on a methane-atmosphered planet. If you'd like, I can introduce you. I know it's not the same, but –". Pastel stopped, since Nebula was shaking her head.

"Right now, we have our hands full with the Orions and Sagittarians. Though someday, I might just try my hand at terraforming."

"Want to go down?" Pastel nodded toward the other side of the ridge.

"Why?"

She did have a point. There seemed to be nothing down that side which wasn't also on the side they had just climbed up.

"Because it's there?" Pastel grinned. And because he yearned to experience the sensory input all over again.

Raised eyebrows was Nebula's only response.

"Well, I'm going down," Flare decided.

"Me, too." Pastel eyed the tropical beach with happy anticipation. "I want to feel the sand between my toes. See you later."

"Don't get lost," Nebula called after them drolly.

Flare's bark of laughter reminded Pastel how much he enjoyed that sound. Not that they didn't express ample mirth in their native form, but there was a lot to be said for a good spontaneous laugh.

It took them a lot less time to reach the beach than it had to climb the hill. Pastel was so eager to savor the twin sensations of sand and surf on his feet that he almost ran down the last part of the hill when the incline became less steep.

They walked the outer edges of the island, splashing through the gentle frothy surf, until Flare and Pastel came upon a secluded cove. A reef further out broke the incoming waves. Small crabs scuttled about their business, paying the humans no mind.

"I don't see any aggressive life forms around." Flare gestured toward the millpond-like stretch of shallow water steaming in the mid-afternoon sun. "Care for a swim?"

Pastel did his own psychic search, which also came up empty. "You bet."

Tepid, refreshing ripples licked ever further up his legs as he waded in. Presently, they were deep enough to swim out a ways from the beach. Pastel dipped his face under and looked downward through the clear, shallow water. Much of the island appeared to be about four feet below the waterline, sloping gradually. The 'shelf' disappeared from view perhaps a quarter-mile offshore.

Pastel alternated between swimming and floating. It felt wonderful to just luxuriate this way, not a care in the world. After a while, he even forgot Flare was nearby. A splash caught his attention, as Flare tipped himself upright and began treading water.

"This has to be the easiest course ever," Flare remarked. "I thought for sure we'd have to sweat it out in some psychic classroom. *This* is what I call sweating!"

"You haven't had Zephyr as a teacher before," Pastel snorted, treading water as well.

For a moment, Flare forgot to move his arms, and started to sink. "Meaning – what?"

"Meaning he starts off easy, and then – *WHAM!*" Pastel slapped the water hard. "A word of advice: Don't get complacent around Zephyr, or he'll get you but good."

Flare shrugged dismissively. "Nebula was no pushover, either. She may look mellow now, but she can be a tyrant when she wants to." He looked around him and sighed. "I hope we get all our lessons here.

"Me, too." Pastel's eyes took in the beauty and the vast array of diversions and recreational opportunities the island and its surrounds afforded them. He could hack the Native Realm in between if he was coming here for their courses. Too bad there wasn't –. "Say, I was just thinking," Pastel said, an idea forming in his mind. "When we get back, maybe I'll try to build something like this. We already made a garden; I don't see why we couldn't make an island and surround it with ocean."

Flare nodded slowly, still looking around him. "Might be fun. I could give you a hand when I'm not busy."

"Great, 'cause I don't know much about creating," Pastel admitted. "What do you think? Should we make it like this, or maybe something fancier?"

"You mean, with caves and stuff? That'd be a nice touch. Maybe even include stalagmites and stalactites. Oh, and Nebula could try her hand at it, too, to see if she'd like to do it 'for real'," Flare added.

Class starts in twenty minutes, Zephyr's mental voice cut in. *Better start back now.*

Pastel chuckled. His wrist now sported a – hopefully waterproof – watch. "Well, there goes *that* excuse." He was feeling better by the minute, but then why shouldn't he? He was *home*.

Together, they waded out of the water and scrambled up the hill, climbing a lot faster than they had coming up the other side. Both were puffing heavily when they reached Zephyr's perch, back atop the rock. Nebula sat beside him, watching them approach.

"You're dripping," she noted. "Shall I dry you off?"

"You can do that?" Pastel blurted out.

Nebula looked surprised he should ask. "Naturally."

"Will that be part of our training?" Flare asked, as instantly, every drop of water on him and Pastel evaporated.

"That depends how many 'recesses' you want," Zephyr needled them before hopping to his feet. "Let's get to work."

Abruptly, the island disappeared and Pastel found himself staring point-blank at an old man as the life force drained from his eyes. Pastel jerked back with a gasp.

Don't let it throw you, Zephyr told him mentally. *Instructors must be unrufflable. As team elder, when all others are blindsided by an event, you must remain focused, able to instantly take control of the situation.*

They were in a hospice, in what was sometimes called the 'dying room'.

"'Abandon hope, all ye who enter here'," Pastel intoned for his companions' ears only. The quote seemed woefully apt, at least from a timespacer point of view.

But why had Zephyr brought them to this place?

Their frocks revealed them to be volunteers, there to provide whatever solace and comfort they could to the dying. At the moment, they were the only staff in the room. The man's precipitous departure had apparently not been anticipated.

"Talk to the others," Zephyr instructed quietly. "But more importantly, *listen* to what they say. Ask them what they are thinking and what questions they have. Don't show an interest in their physical well-being; they have none. What they do have is a permanent existence they know nothing about."

"Can we tell them about it?" Pastel asked, just above a whisper.

Zephyr shrugged. "Depends. Use your own judgment, but err on the side of kindness. For some, it would upset their beliefs, and them with it. This close to departure, if in doubt, leave them with their illusions. They'll know soon enough, and then it won't matter."

There were five people in the room. The two who caught Pastel's eye were so decrepit and emaciated with age that he wondered how they could still be 'alive'. They were in separate beds, side-by-side, but holding hands across the small divide. Theirs were the eyes of a pair-bond which had withstood everything human life could throw at them and fearlessly faced the end together, with dignity.

Their warmth was almost palpable. Pastel hurried towards their bedsides.

"Hello, dear hearts." As he looked from one to the other, Pastel knew he had a foolish grin on his face, but he couldn't help it. "Do you know that your love warms this room? We haven't had to turn on the heat since you arrived."

"What a sweet thing to say," the woman exclaimed.

Her mate squinted at Pastel. "These old eyes ain't what they used to be, but I don't remember seeing you before. New, are you?"

"Well, in a manner of speaking . . ."

The woman squeezed her husband's hand and grinned wickedly at Pastel. "Bet you'll stick around longer'n we will. We're planning on going together, George 'n me."

Pastel realized he was being gently teased, as though they were trying to prepare *him* for the shock of their passing.

"And we'll *stay* together, Martha, no matter what," the man said firmly. "That I promise."

"Yes, we will." Martha smiled at her husband before turning to Pastel. "So don't you fret about us when we're gone. Manys the time we didn't know where we were going, but we always got there alright, didn't we, George?"

"Always."

A terrible hacking cough tore through the old man's wasted body, and for a tense moment Pastel thought George would expire on the spot. Eventually, he reopened his eyes.

"Thought I was a goner, didn't ya?" he chuckled. "Don't let it throw ya, son. We all gotta go sometime, but not everyone's got such good company." His gnarled fingers rubbed the back of his wife's hand to reinforce the compliment.

To his consternation, Pastel felt tears well up in his eyes. He grinned sheepishly at the couple. "Silly me. I always get this way around love stories. Can you give me a minute? I'll be right back."

Pastel brushed the tears away and approached Zephyr, who was holding a middle-aged bald-headed woman's too-white hand. The octogenarian appeared to be sleeping peacefully. Zephyr raised his eyebrows in pointed reference to Pastel's tears.

"It's that old couple. They're just so wonderful," Pastel stammered. "Can I show them what we are, so they *know* they'll always be together?"

Zephyr glanced in their direction, then shrugged noncommittally. "They already know, but go ahead if you want. Just don't let the others see it."

"Thanks, boss." Pastel flashed Zephyr a grateful smile before retracing his steps. He drew the curtain and turned to face their looks of surprise.

"I've been given permission to show you something." He turned up his energy level until his body glowed and vibrated from the added input. Although he was carefully controlling the flow, the intensity made him catch his breath.

George's eyes grew wide, and his toothless mouth flew open. "Martha, do you see that?"

"You mean that light around him? Yes!" She gazed at Pastel with lively interest and not a shred of fear. "Who might you be, young man? Or *are* you a man?"

Pastel allowed the last of the excess energy to leach from his body.

"Not really. I'm what you are when you're not being human." Pastel nodded toward the rest of his party, now hidden by the curtain. "And so are my colleagues. Actually, our instructor brought us here as part of our training."

Martha's cracked lips pursed prettily. "An angel-in-training, then?"

"No, we're not angels." Pastel waggled a hand. "More like beings who design, create and tend universes and the like. We all have our own specialties, but we can change careers whenever we like."

"So, what do you do, exactly?" Martha wanted to know.

After all the times Pastel had answered that timespacer question, the answer rolled off his tongue without him having to think about it. "My colleagues and I answer any human who calls home. Most of us also take 'working vacations' in time-space. It helps us remember what it's like to be immersed in a virtual reality." Then he diverged from the 'script' to add, "And like you two are doing, soulmates often travel together."

George gave a little whoop. "Hey-hey-hey! I *told* you we'd stay together. I *knew* it; I just knew it!"

"We both did," Martha assured him, eyes twinkling. "Love is eternal. Isn't that right, Mr. ah –"

Pastel shifted his feet self-consciously. "We don't *actually* have names; we don't need them. But those of us who time-space a lot sometimes call ourselves things . . ."

"And yours is?" Martha prodded, her rheumy eyes twinkling merrily.

"Cool Pastel. 'Pastel' for short," he supplied, feeling very foolish indeed.

"Pleased to meetcha," George nodded.

Martha gazed at Pastel, her face glowing with eager intensity. There was something she fervently wanted to know, he realized, and was afraid he'd vanish before she found out. "Tell me, Pastel.

156

Have we –" her bony finger traveled between her and her husband. "– uh, time-spaced before?"

"Many, many times," Pastel smiled softly. He knew what she was about to ask, but had only just recognized true-them in this, their current embodiment. They had never called the Helpline in this lifetime.

"What names do we call ourselves there?" she asked.

Seeing them in the flesh – or what little was left on their bones – Pastel could hardly contain his mirth, for their pseudonyms suited their personalities to a 'T'. He pointed first to Martha, then to George. "Peaches and Cream."

Martha's free hand flew to her mouth, which she covered in a self-conscious giggle. "No! You're not serious?"

George cackled gleefully. "I've always loved *peaches,* my luscious.*"

"Oh, stop that!" Martha pinked with pleasure.

Zephyr's discreet throat-clearing told Pastel it was time to leave.

"I must go now, friends," he said, giving their frail hands the tiniest squeeze. "I happen to know you'll both have an easy transition. I'll see you soon, at home." At least he hoped they would arrive before he left for good. He couldn't resist adding, as he pulled back the curtain. "With a big bowl of peaches and cream."

"We'll hold you to that," Martha called to his departing back.

"Well done," Zephyr said quietly, as Pastel rejoined the group. "For a while there, I thought you wouldn't recognize them."

"I nearly didn't. They're so in love, I was beguiled."

"Unsurprisingly," was Zephyr's less-than-subtle dig.

Pastel looked back wistfully toward the elderly couple. As he turned away, the room dissolved to black.

CHAPTER 7

"Where are we?" Pastel asked.

If Zephyr was present, he didn't answer. Pastel could have reached out mentally and checked, but he felt certain they were all in the same location. It was pitch black; not the slightest hint of light penetrated their location. His words had echoed slightly, so Pastel realized they were in a room, one that held little or no furniture. He could feel a wooden floor beneath him. There was a slight residual chemical odor which he thought he recognized.

"I think it's a photographic darkroom," Flare ventured, as Pastel opened his mouth to speak.

"Correct," Zephyr confirmed. "This is a vacant house. The room is empty, and the electricity has been turned off. It was one of the darkest unfurnished enclosed places I could find above-ground. What time is it, Flare?" Zephyr asked.

"I don't know."

"Pastel, what day and year?"

Pastel thought he knew where Zephyr was going with this, but played along. "No idea."

"What country or city, Nebula?"

She projected a mental shrug.

"And if you hadn't identified the room by smell, Flare, you wouldn't even know if you were still on Earth or in the bowels of some carrier in space. Time and spacial awareness are how the outfocused orient themselves. They depend on that input for their decisions. Everything they do, think, feel, express and experience is relative to someone or something else. Which means, their decisions are usually dictated or at least influenced by something outside of themselves."

That's hardly news, Pastel thought. *What is he getting at?*

Zephyr's voice bounced subtly off the walls, giving his rich tone a haunting quality. "Here in the dark, the first thing you all did was try to glean as much information about your surroundings as you could. You felt the floor beneath you, sniffed the air for clues, noted the ambient temperature and humidity. From that you determined you were in a room. Then some of you mentally verified that the rest of us were present, while others –" he paused significantly. "*Assumed* I would have kept us all together. I wouldn't make any such assumptions, if I were you.

If I asked you now to get us out of here, Flare, what would you do?"

"Find the door."

"Pastel?"

He nodded, even though the others couldn't see it. "I agree. It would be easier to find in the dark than a light switch, even if you hadn't told us the power was off."

"Nebula?"

Humor tinged her response. "Teleport us out the same way you got us in."

Pastel was glad no one could see him wince. Caught again. Only this time, he hadn't been alone. He found himself casting about for at least a glimmer of light. He had always avoided dark places, and liked it even less in the company of Zephyr-the-Unpredictable.

If their instructor felt Pastel's growing discomfiture, he ignored it. "When your callers are in the dark, or blinded by their problems and are casting around for a way out, remember how quickly you forgot the obvious and became caught up in appearances. Sometimes, 'you don't have to fight the alligators'; you can simply leave the swamp."

"Yes, but most timespacers take their 'swamp' with them, wherever they go," Pastel pointed out. "If they could leave it behind that easily, they probably wouldn't be in the mess they're in in the first place." He was rather surprised Zephyr, of all people, hadn't considered that.

"Your point is valid, as far as it goes," Zephyr agreed. "But to keep from drawing the same experiences again and again, people first must recognize the theme they are living out – their personal black hole, shall we say. They have to realize they are drawing these scenarios, or being drawn into them, and why. Few can do so while immersed in them. They need to step outside the story to see it for what it is. To 'leave the swamp', however briefly, gives them the lead time to identify their life theme from without and make a new, feelinged decision about 'where to from here'. Otherwise, yes, they would almost certainly mire themselves in yet another swamp."

Pastel risked a light probe, but couldn't detect any trace of censure in Zephyr's reply. Did Zephyr, then, not realize Pastel planned to leave his own personal black hole, his 'swamp'? Had Pastel, after all, been able to hide it from his keenly-aware instructor? And even more surprising, if Zephyr didn't know, that meant Murmur had kept Pastel's scheme a secret. His relief morphed into shock. If she hadn't told Zephyr, there could only be one reason: *Murmur* wanted *Pastel to leave!*

"That's it for here, folks," Zephyr was saying. "Nebula, do the honors, please."

Pastel scrambled to pull his wits back around him before they relocated. For the moment, he was 'outside his swamp', to some extent. He relived in fast-forward his shameful behavior when Murmur found him in the garden, wallowing in self-pity, how he'd blown up at her before she could even say a word. Pastel's intestines knotted like a pretzel. He couldn't blame Murmur – or Memory, for that matter – for wanting him gone. There in the dark, Pastel nodded once, decisively, as the final mote of ambivalence vanished. As soon as his training was complete, he would honor their wishes, as well as his own, and disappear for all eternity.

"Where to and when?" Nebula inquired.

"Your choice," Zephyr replied, adding, "And while you're at it, choose and teach the next lesson, if you will."

Pastel braced himself for yet another abrupt change of venue, but it was the last thing he would have expected. They were sitting in uncomfortable seats at the back of an elementary school classroom – and their bodies were about twelve years old.

*

Well, at least we kept our genders, Pastel thought. To switch in midstream would have been unnerving, though there were no guarantees Zephyr wouldn't pull that stunt on them later.

Once again, Pastel experienced a sense of inner peace but more so, now that his decision to depart had been made on an objective as well as an emotional level. He felt subtly separate from his colleagues. Pastel's gaze lingered briefly on his instructor. How would his defection from nonspace affect Zephyr? Would it cause him guilt or, worse yet, possibly taint his career? Pastel fervently hoped not. He owed his instructor a lot, if only for putting up with Pastel all this time. He resolved to excel in everything he was being taught, as much as a tribute to Zephyr as to cement his own plans.

Pastel scanned the room and noticed with surprise that no one was looking at them. "Are we visible?" he whispered.

"Only to each other," Nebula replied out loud. "Nor can they hear us. I suggest you concentrate on the lesson and what is being learned."

". . . assignment is to draw our solar system. Then write down what each planet is like, what makes it different from all the rest, and why only Earth currently supports life."

A collective groan of protest rose from the students. The teacher ignored it, raising her voice to be heard. "It must be no less than 500 words, and it's due Thursday, February 12th. That's two weeks from today."

"But we have a big chemistry thing due then, and it'll take forever," a boy wailed. "Can't you make it the week after?"

A swell of support for that idea gathered momentum, as the teacher was seen to hesitate.

Finally, she raised her hands. "Alright, alright, settle down. Very well; you have until February 19th to hand it in, but –" She looked around the room sternly, making eye contact with those who, Pastel felt certain, were the slackers in the group. "I expect quality work from each one of you. No copying off the Internet or from textbooks. I want everything in your own words."

The bell rang then, and the children and teacher gathered up their belongings in preparation for their next class. Soon only the Helpliners remained in the room.

"What was so special about that?" Flare asked.

Nebula shook her head, long hair now in pigtails. "Nothing in itself. But there was something significant being taught and learned. What was it?"

"Whining pays off?" Flare offered.

"That is discovered in infancy. Think subliminal," Nebula prompted.

Zephyr's expression gave nothing away. Pastel replayed the short scene, frowning in concentration. The teacher had only done what teachers do: teach and assign homework which –

"Hang on," Pastel exclaimed. "I was just thinking, 'teachers assign homework which has to be done by a certain date'. But the important part of that is *'which has to be done'*, right?"

Nebula's adolescent face broke into a comely smile. "Right. Obedience stems from the belief that the person *has no choice*. And that goes for most things in the average human's life. Whether they are children, adults, spouses, parents, seniors, employees or, ultimately, facing 'death', most of what they do is because they believe they have no alternative. Yet what is the cornerstone of time-space trips?"

"Options," Pastel and Flare said in unison.

"When your callers say 'I can't do this' or 'I have to do that', they are really saying 'I have no choice'. Options right under their nose are invisible to them because they don't believe they *have* any. Which is why, as Helpliners, we point out options, and at every turn seed opportunities for them to change their mind if they want to."

Flare looked glum. "But almost none of them do."

Nebula shrugged. "It's their adventure; it's their right to seek solutions or accept their perceived limitations. But another lesson was being learned as well, that neither of you have mentioned yet . . .". She gazed expectantly at Pastel and Flare.

Zephyr, Pastel noticed, was trying to keep his expression neutral, but his eyes gleamed knowingly. Apparently, Zephyr had picked up something which he felt Nebula had missed, but she hadn't after all.

"A hint," Nebula offered. "It has to do with what the teacher said at the end."

Pastel scanned his memory. She had said she wanted 500 words or more, in their own words, not copied . . . Pastel was diving for a deeper meaning when Flare said triumphantly "Oh, of course!"

A wisp of a smile curled the corners of Nebula's fine lips. "Go ahead."

"She said 'I expect quality work from each one of you.' The crux of that was expectations, right?" Flare raised his eyebrows, drolly daring her to deny it.

"Correct. When those perceived to be in authority over others (in this case a teacher over her students) states an expectation, the underlings will try to fulfill it or avoid fulfilling it. Either way, it keeps them focused on the teacher, rather than on themselves. And of course, expectations can be negative as well. Timespacers are constantly living up to or down to other people's expectations of them.

Let's look at what happens if people consider someone a low-life . . ."

Pastel barely managed to suppress a gasp. He'd very recently called himself that. Did Nebula know or was her choice of words a bizarre coincidence?

". . . that person will either try to prove them wrong or, if he believes that he is, then he'll strive to prove them right. The other way this can play out is that he'll do the same based not on what others think of him, but what he *thinks* their perception of him is, and oftentimes he's absolutely wrong. Regardless, it keeps him focused on them and their expectations, real or imagined.

But, there's a third option." Nebula paused significantly. "He can do what he sees fit, with no association between it and anyone else's perspectives of him. That third option is seldom recognized and therefore rarely used. That's why most people live their whole lives in relation to others, playing to other people or playing in other people's games rather than their own." She then turned a quizzical eye on Zephyr, mutely indicating the 'lesson' was over.

"Ready to go?" Zephyr inquired.

They all pried themselves out of the seats, and Pastel mentally prepared himself for their next venue. The new location came as both a relief and a disappointment: They were back in their Native Realm.

CHAPTER 8

Pastel was still trying to figure exactly where in nonspace he had been dropped off when he got the call.

Pastel, are you free?

He masked his surprise that she would contact him, after the way he had acted. Feigning nonchalance, Pastel transmitted, *I think so. Why?*

I could really use your help.

Memory was easy to locate, with her broadcasting frustration as much as she was. At least this time it wasn't directed at him, and Pastel was only too glad to forget the past. He placed his essence alongside her on the garden bench.

"Problem?"

Memory nodded, and silently produced a psychic recording. "What's wrong with this answer?"

"What was the question, first?" Pastel interjected, as Memory moved to activate the device.

"Okay, I'll replay it from the beginning. I took an extra shift with Team 2, and I thought I was doing so well, when all of a sudden Fjord mentally pushed me aside and took over the call," Memory said indignantly. "And afterwards, he wouldn't tell me why; he just said 'research faults'."

"Faults, huh? Let's see what you've got."

Memory triggered the recording.

Maybe this is a silly question, but try as I might, I cannot remove all my faults. Is it even *possible* to have no character flaws?

Pastel recognized the 'voice' of Wise Acre, aka Cindy, the sage. Switzerland, late 18th Century.

Probably not. But since everyone in your society is expected to have some, why not deliberately replace those you don't want with ones which will give you the most entertainment value?

Memory stopped the recording to say defensively, "Well, it makes sense, doesn't it? People choose lifetimes to explore different things, not always ones their society approves of. Anyway, what's considered a fault in one culture is a respected asset in another; you know that."

"We do, but Cindy doesn't," Pastel pointed out. "She has no memory of the other civilizations and eras she's lived in, with their vastly different values and beliefs. Your response was – if you'll pardon the pun – honest to a fault. And to her, where she is now and based on what she's trying to do, it amounts to misinformation."

Memory bristled, red sparks shooting to the edges of her aura. "So what was I supposed to tell her? That they're bad and must be removed? Most outfocused are *deliberately* exploring what happens when they live out damaging beliefs or faults. Calling them 'wrong' would not only be hypocritical, it would be an out-and-out lie. And I wouldn't lie to her even if we were allowed to."

Pastel could empathize, having run up against the same problem repeatedly. "No one's suggesting you lie, but there other are ways to get around the question. Most timespacers aren't looking for a full dissertation on a topic, Memory; they just want a quick explanation – or more often, a quick fix. She was speaking in code. For 'Is it possible to not have faults?' read 'How can I become a better person?'. She's a sage, remember. People depend on her to set an example, to be 'wise and all-knowing'. Chances are, there is one main concept plaguing her. Find out what it is and help her put it in perspective. She'll do the rest, if she's at all serious."

"Oh, I get it. Just because she asked a blanket question doesn't mean wants an overview answer." With that, Memory's aura brightened noticeably.

Pastel exuded approval and reassurance, surreptitiously nudging it in her direction. "Exactly. I suggest you record what you would say if you were asked that same question again, then show it to Fjord and get his feedback."

"I will. Thanks for your help. And Pastel?" She rubbed his aura tentatively. "I'm sorry I came down on you like that. I didn't understand about addictions."

Pastel imaged a shake of a head. "Don't apologize; I had it coming – that and a lot worse."

Memory arced herself into a Cheshire catlike grin and summarily disappeared.

Zephyr? Pastel transmitted. *When am I due on the Helpline?*

Turned out Pastel had a long stretch of free-range time, having worked through three breaks while they were on course.

Perfect time to get started on his island-building project. It would keep him busy between Helpline stints and courses and, he realized, would make an excellent parting gift. But he couldn't do it alone. Whisper was far too busy to help him with it, but the Life Properties Infuser might have connections who could.

"How did it go?", the LPI asked when Pastel materialized beside him. Whisper was scrutinizing twin moons of a gigantic water planet.

"Remarkable and exhausting," Pastel admitted. "Zephyr took us to Earth, like he said he would. In fully-functional human bodies, no less."

Whisper stopped what he was doing to ask cryptically, "When and where?"

"We spent most of our time on this lovely tropic isle – south Pacific, I think. Absolutely pristine and no other land in sight, so I've no idea when. Funny thing is, the last few lifetimes I never got near the water, and I'd almost forgotten how much I love to swim. I want to build an island like that right here, with acres of ocean around it."

Whisper dismissed the panoramic view of the planet and moons. "It would be fun to do as a project, but I don't see the point of having an ocean. Without a body here, you couldn't swim anyway."

"Maybe I don't need one. Granted it'll be a challenge, but we can extrude arm and leg-like appendages, so why couldn't we use them to swim?" Pastel argued.

Negative vibes radiated from Whisper, as he said, "No way. Not weightless like we are."

He did have a point. But Pastel wasn't about to let that bit of logic stand in the way of his goal. "One of the things we were reminded in this course was how quickly humans accept limitations as insurmountable. Nothing's impossible if you want it badly enough."

"Maybe." Whisper gazed at him silently just long enough to put Pastel on his guard before he said, his mental voice carefully neutral. "Let's say you could make a body. Considering recent events, are you sure it's wise? You've been getting caught up in human perspectives a lot lately, you know."

Pastel grimaced, less from the reminder than realizing he'd have to tell his friend that he was leaving. But not yet; not till he was ready to go.

"I'm not saying it *would* be a problem," Whisper temporized. "Just that it *might* be. Still," he projected a wistful look. "A tropic island would be a great addition to this place."

Pastel pounced on the admission. "You mean you'd go there? If we had one?"

"In a heartbeat! If I had one."

"I didn't think you'd be interested."

Whisper said, his 'voice' reduced to a conspiratorial level, "To be honest, this is home and all, but sometimes it gets a bit boring. It's too predictable."

"You know what would be neat?" Ideas sprouted in Pastel's mind like weeds. "A whole *series* of leisure spots from different worlds – different galaxies and universes, even! Or maybe, take elements from all sorts of planets and put them together to make a completely new environment. The possibilities are endless –"

Whisper interrupted to say, "What you're getting so fired up about is exactly what Terraformers and Spacial Phenomena Specialists do – only for real."

"That's true. Got any contacts among them?"

"Me? No."

Belatedly, Pastel realized he hadn't even asked about Whisper's new project. "So, um, what are you planning with those moons?"

Whisper expelled a knowing snort. "Go see the specialists first. I'll tell you when I can hold your attention on it for more than a nanosecond." He gave Pastel a good-natured shove.

"Okay," Pastel smiled as he relocated. Whisper was right; Pastel hadn't felt this much enthusiasm since he joined the Helpline.

*

The SPS contingent had fashioned an imaginative panorama for their test center. As far as Pastel cared to look, there were plants, shrubs, grasses and trees of every description, on long, low tables. Spacial Phenomena Specialists worked diligently at a number of these platforms.

Before Pastel had time to wonder how he should introduce himself, a mental welcome invited him to enter. All around him, SPS workers transmitted greetings, and one being came towards him. Pastel felt a shock of recognition. It was Murmur. But what was *she* doing here?

"I didn't know you liked flora enough to come here," she said by way of greeting. "But then, it was your idea to make that garden, so why am I surprised?"

Pastel hadn't realized it either, until just now. He found himself staring at one plant, tree or flower after another, amazed at how many permutations on the basic theme of plant life there were. "Well, I don't have a green thumb, or anything," he admitted. "I guess I just like looking at them. But what about you? When did you develop such an interest in plants?"

"Last time-space trip, I took a couple courses in botany, remember?" Murmur said, as she led him through the winding path between workstations until they arrived at hers. On her bench was a delicate-looking flower that seemed to reflect light in a way no blossom Pastel had ever seen could.

He bent forward for a closer look. "That's true. So, is this your new project?"

"I volunteer here once in a while. I find it relaxing. This is a pre-organic crystal flower. The challenge is to have it retain its structural integrity from bud to blossom."

Pastel peered deep inside the multi-faceted living gemflower. It seemed to trap light within, emitting a soft, inviting glow from the bloom's core.

"Insects will be drawn into the center, where the crystalline dust will adhere to them for pollination," Murmur explained. "I'm building in a light-retention system so it will attract insects even on overcast days."

Pastel was unable to take his focus off the intricate facets. "It's exquisite. I had no idea you had such a creative flair! Do you have a planet in mind for it?"

"No; that's not our job. This section designs new basic flora. What you see here is just an extrapolation of what this flower *might* eventually look like, at one stage of its evolution. But that will depend on the environment into which it is inserted. The Ecologists will be seeding a very primitive ancestor of this."

"I never realized there were so many variables in creating," Pastel said, greatly impressed.

Murmur gave the flower a final tweak, then straightened up. "Don't take this the wrong way, because I'm very glad to see you, but – why are you here?"

Pastel hesitated, as he looked around him. "When you're finished your stint –"

"I just did," Murmur smiled.

"Can we go someplace private to talk? It's about a project I have in mind."

Her smile widened. "*Well!* I definitely have time for that. Follow me." And she teleported out of sight.

Pastel felt her mindprint just beyond the opposite side of the SPS department. When he closed in on her location, he spotted something that resembled a giant weeping willow tree. Only, the cascading boughs appeared to be composed of magnificent plumes of fiery red and brilliant yellow hair flowing to the base of the trunk. Pastel headed towards the arboreal wonder. He quickened his progress when a section of the plumes parted to reveal a beckoning Murmur. Soft filaments tickled Pastel as the Helpliner moved through the hairy barrier. Inside, the colors were muted, the atmosphere intimate and inviting.

"Your creation?" He couldn't help but marvel at the spaciousness as well as the ambiance.

"One of my first. Do you like it?"

Pastel found himself at a loss for words.

Murmur chuckled. "I'll take that as a yes."

"A most *definite* yes," he assured her.

Murmur materialized a pair of soft surround-chairs and positioned her essence onto the one nearest her. "So tell me about this project."

Pastel began describing the island he had just been on, which led easily into his project and the purpose of his visit to the SPS department. "I'd like to make it a self-contained ecosystem, same as our garden. This would be much more complex, of course, and I'll need plenty of help. You wouldn't have time, perhaps . . .?"

"I'll *make* time!" Murmur assured him. "This'd be a botanical dream-job. Count me in."

Pastel found himself beaming foolishly. To have most of his free time here spent in her company was an unexpected and most wonderful bonus, and he intended to take full advantage of it. "So the next question is, who else should we rope in?"

"Well, we'll need a Terraformer, of course, and an Aquatic Specialist to handle the ocean part."

Which brought to Pastel's mind another possibility. "Before we go any further, we should decide: Do we want fauna?"

Murmur leaned back as she often did when thinking. "I don't know. Spaceform rocks and plants and water is one thing. But there'd be a lot more programming involved in creating mock mobile life forms."

"No fauna, then," Pastel decided. "But we'll need an Ecologist to balance the whole system so it remains active and is self-sustaining. Got any contacts in those areas?"

Murmur nodded. "I think I know one Aquarian and an Ecologist team who'd be willing to have a busman's holiday. But a Terraformer – no; I've never met one."

"Any idea where they hang out?"

She projected a shake of the head, without actually extruding a pseudo-head.

"Sorry. Wouldn't your friend Whisper know?"

"If he does, he's never mentioned it. Hang on a sec."

Pastel beamed his query to Whisper, who was unsuccessful in masking a momentary annoyance. The interruption had caught him at a crucial moment in his work. Pastel transmitted a hasty apology and was about to withdraw when Whisper stopped him, curious now.

"What's up?"

"How much time do you have?" Pastel countered. He wasn't about to further irritate his friend.

Pastel felt Whisper's focus sharpen. "The project? You're starting already?"

"Not quite." Which led to as succinct as possible a description of what he and Murmur had been discussing, and the reason for Pastel's 'call'. "You work on planets and such likes which haven't got any life on them yet, so we figured you might know the Terraformers who made them in the first place."

"Surprisingly, no, I don't. And there's another set of nursers like the ones who monitor my life infusions. Only they do that with the newly-formed planets, from the time they coalesce from what humans call 'star material' to when they're stable enough for me and my colleagues to work on. Accelerated greatly, of course. But I haven't met them, either. Sorry."

Pastel thanked him and apologized again before telling Murmur, "No go. So I guess it's up to us – for now, anyway."

Ideas and counter-suggestions came thick and fast, and Pastel reveled in the chance to interact with Murmur – dare he even think it? – more intimately than he had been able to on the Helpline. Finally, there seemed nothing more they could do until they put their team together.

"If you can interest the other specialists you mentioned, I'll try to snag us a Terraformer," Pastel said, as they were getting ready to leave.

"Will do. And since you seem to like my Tree, let's meet here to compare notes, when we finish rounding up the others – oops. You're being paged. See you later."

As she winked away, he opened up to Whisper, surprised to hear from him so soon. Pastel realized with a start how long that brainstorming session with Murmur had lasted.

"I might have goofed a bit." It was Whisper's turn to sound apologetic.

"Oh? How so?"

Whisper said quietly, as though afraid to be overheard. "Had you been planning to keep the island thing a secret?"

"No. As a matter of fact, Murmur and I are out drumming up help. Why?"

A *whoosh* of relief washed over Pastel.

"Oh, good. I sort of mentioned it to a couple of my colleagues, and I guess they passed it on, because suddenly I'm getting swamped with questions I can't answer, like when the island will be done and how many people it'll hold. It feels like half of nonspace has heard of it already and wants to 'party'."

Pastel didn't quite know what to say. "But . . . we haven't even begun yet."

"Then I suggest you get at it, like right now."

Pastel scowled as Whisper's mental touch vanished from his mind. Pressure! Just what he didn't need more of right now.

But on the positive side, at least now he knew his gift would be used.

Pastel put his future plans aside for the moment and set off to find a Terraformer. Rumor had it that 'rock hounds' were an unruly lot, delighting in unconventionality. Pastel supposed that, if he spent so much time molding planets, he'd be a bit spinny, too. Come to think of it, he was. Still, Pastel approached their domain with some trepidation.

"Looking for a Terraformer for your little project, are you?" a merry voice boomed.

Pastel gaped at the burly being who came forward to greet him. "How did you know?"

"We have our sources. Nothing much goes on we don't hear about. Like you splitting in Streak and being trained by a psyche, no less! You're famous, m'boy. Or should I say, 'infamous'?" He made Pastel a motion. "Don't just stand there gawking. Come on in. We don't bite, despite what people may think."

The effusive fellow seemed unlikely to stop his monologue any time soon. Pastel followed him into a landscape of scaled-down mountain ranges, steep gorges and expansive valleys, some of which were being acted upon by speeded-up glacial flows. The model they were facing sported a greenish atmosphere of swirling gases and hurricane-force winds.

"Inhospitable, wouldn't you say?" the Terraformer asked conversationally, as he observed the model Pastel was gaping at. "But the creatures destined for this planet will call it home. They will consider it paradise. And do you know why? Because they will be perfectly adapted to their environment. That's the key, m'boy: compatibility. They will adapt to their environment, and adapt their environment to them. End result? A perfect fit. Which is why there's such stiff competition in our happy midst –". He motioned toward a group of Terraformers looking interestedly in their direction. "– over who gets to work on your little diversion."

Pastel couldn't believe his nonexistent ears. "There is? I thought I'd have to *beg*. I mean, this is your job. Why would you want to do it between shifts?"

"Because the lucky 'Former can work on the project as a whole, molding it to the flora as well as the other way around. *And I hear tell you want to use elements and plants from a variety of worlds. Now, that's going to be some challenge! Best of all, no one's schedule will be thrown off if we experiment a bit.*"

"No, indeed. It's strictly for fun," Pastel assured him.

The Terraformer sighed wistfully. "I guess the only fair way is to 'draw straws' or some such. But between you and me, I'd love to stack the deck in my favor," he grinned, blithely mixing metaphors.

Pastel extruded a pseudofinger to poke into the eye of the hurricane. "Why not just take turns? Whoever's off-shift and wants to help can pitch in. We'll keep a running tally of what's being done or considered, so the next person can pick up where the last one left off."

The Terraformer leaked doubt. "You could end up with the most cockeyed island ever conceived."

"Or it could be the most imaginative," Pastel countered. "And if it doesn't work out, we can always start over or replace the parts that don't fit. I'll run it by Murmur and let you know when we're ready to start."

"Good-o."

Pastel left, already mulling over some unexpected revelations. Lately, it seemed everyone he met had timespaced as a human at least once. This talkative fellow certainly had, considering his choice of expressions. What was there about being human which made it so popular? Or was it the planet itself?

The important thing is, Pastel reminded himself, *we now have Terraformers.*

"And I've snared the Ecologist couple and the help of my favorite Aquarian," Murmur transmitted, inserting the thought smoothly into Pastel's ruminations.

"Excellent! Then it looks like we're in business. Are you free?" Pastel transmitted back.

"Just about. Meet you under our Tree."

Our Tree? Pastel liked the sound of that. He relocated to 'their' arboreal oasis, smiling in anticipation. The creative juices were flowing, bringing forth a host of tantalizing images. He visualized a deep pool warmed by hot springs and fed by a three-tiered waterfall; multi-hued flowers cascading down from shade trees, their fragrance sensually perfuming the air.

"Romantic!" Murmur smiled, appearing so close to Pastel that their auras almost overlapped. She was carrying a gigantic book of mind-pictures.

"What are these?"

Murmur took a moment to merge the two surround-chairs into one half-moon loveseat that would fit both of them comfortably. "Flora. I've brought a few million samples. Care to browse?"

"Aren't you the thoughtful soul?"

The plant life Murmur had chosen ranged from the intricate and spectacular to subdued carpets of moss, from bizarre shapes to symmetrical perfection – all in an astounding variety of textures and hues.

"I don't know where to begin," Pastel exclaimed, overwhelmed. "The SPS made all these?"

Murmur laughed indulgently. "And they don't even scratch the surface. Remember, the SPS have been in operation since the concept of time-space was first introduced. And not all their creations get used – not by a long shot. The Ecologists pick and choose, and the rest remain as options for other projects."

Pastel stared at Murmur in wonder. "How do they – and you – keep track of them all?"

"You worked at the library. How did *you* keep track of all that data?" Murmur asked rhetorically.

Pastel 'thumbed' through the pages of images. "So, any of these could be used on our little island? They would fit together?"

"Well, some better than others," she admitted. "But I'd recommend we make it a *big* island. The word is spreading like wildfire. It seems everyone I know (and plenty I've never met) are inundating me with questions and their own pet requests."

Pastel nodded. "Whisper, too. He got the rumor-mill going."

"And I think I fueled it. We may have to build a second one. But for now, let's start with a baseline visual for the first."

*

"Why are you surprised?" the psyche asked Zephyr. "You must know by now to expect the unexpected from that source."

"From Pastel, yes. But this is from many others as well."

"We don't live in a vacuum here, socially speaking, any more than the outfocused do in their time-space worlds. There were bound to be repercussions, and what you are seeing is just the beginning. This trend needs to be encouraged, not contained. Such events are the birthplace of exponential growth and change."

Zephyr projected a solemn nod. "Then I will stimulate it all I can."

*

When Pastel got a call from Zephyr, some time later, he assumed another course was about to begin.

"Not yet," Zephyr told Pastel when he arrived. "It's about your island."

Pastel waited for the elder to elaborate, wondering if Zephyr, too, wanted in on the project. During his meeting with Murmur, they had been deluged by incoming calls.

"You seem to have generated a lot of interest in terrestrial diversions. Because of that, we're getting a flood of requests to outfocus."

"Uh . . ." Pastel didn't know whether Zephyr considered that good or not.

"Very good indeed," Zephyr assured him, obviously knowing his thoughts. "And that includes many who have never timespaced before. It will add enormously to our learning curve, but it also presents a few problems."

Pastel nodded his understanding. "Like having enough Helpliners to go around."

"Precisely. So many want to outfocus that we'll have to at least quadruple our ranks to handle them all. That means more trainees and," Zephyr paused significantly. "More trainers."

With a sinking feeling, Pastel reached the conclusion Zephyr had pointedly left unspoken. "I won't have time to work on the island, will I?"

"And Nebula cannot be spared for the Helpline, either; her instructor services are too badly needed," Zephyr said, indirectly confirming Pastel's suspicion. "It's ironic, really. Your idea is so good that it's cutting you out of the picture. But we simply can't leave timespacers to manage on their own without backup."

Pastel sighed heavily. "No. But how can we handle that many? Even if I *were* fully trained – which I'm not – that would only make three instructors for this sector. Unless the other elders are qualified to teach?" Pastel looked at Zephyr hopefully.

"Most aren't."

"About how long does it take to get a Helpliner to instructor level?"

Zephyr brought his mind to bear, so that Pastel could not doubt the seriousness of his words. "At the intensity I intend to proceed with you and the other recruits, you will quickly become qualified."

Pastel gulped, but not at the implied threat. Deep within, his sense of fairness was squirming. Here he was, letting himself be trained with no intention of remaining to help out. Yet every instructor would be desperately needed, because of Pastel. He intended to forsake Zephyr and the outfocused when they needed him most, just to protect Murmur and fulfill his own selfish needs. The line between martyrdom at best and treason at worst was growing exceedingly fine.

"How *many* other recruits?", Pastel asked, grasping at the one possible bright spot in what his instructor had said.

At that moment, for a high-energy being, Zephyr actually looked tired. "I had to beg, coerce and bribe shamelessly, but I did manage to commandeer enough former Helpliners to stand in for those like you who are willing to upgrade. The elders will monitor the formers, as their skills are bound to be rusty. That's the best we can do."

Pastel winced. "I'm sorry. If I'd known . . ."

But Zephyr waved it off. "Don't let it throw you. We may have to scramble now, but it will pay off handsomely in the long run."

"How many Helpliners are upgrading?"

"If none change their mind, eight – which should be just enough to train the recruits we need. But we have to factor in possible dropouts or ones who just don't have what it takes. Instructing isn't for everyone, and this 'crash course' will be tough. But I did mention bribery . . ."

Pastel squirmed at the thought of being rewarded, considering his ulterior motive, but there was no way to refuse it without raising suspicion.

"During the few short breaks," Zephyr was saying, "A substitute will stand in for close friends and mates so that they can join the trainees if they wish."

"Most thoughtful," Pastel said, though he realized Zephyr could also have an ulterior motive. A rest break with friends and loved-ones was bound to 'recharge the batteries' more quickly than any other form of R&R.

"Quite so," Zephyr agreed, as usual responding to Pastel's surface thoughts. "But the second concession is virtually unprecedented: The psyches will increase your energy mass, and that of your fellow students, to sustain each of you more comfortably."

"Wow!" Pastel was silent for a moment. He remembered the supercharged feeling he had experienced during Streak. "Will you receive more, too?"

"Mercifully, yes. There is one other thing you must understand: Under the workload, tempers are bound to fray. You must not feel – or let anyone make you feel – the least bit guilty for this little crisis. By stimulating such an increased interest in timespacing, you have unwittingly touched off an evolution revolution – or so the psyches tell me. True, some trainees will be inconvenienced, but over time, the more outfocusing that is done, the more we learn and the faster we progress. Also –"

Pastel imaged a staying hand. "Hang on a sec. If you want people to outfocus more, why am I not allowed to? Why place a limit on the number of times we can go?"

"Because it's supposed to help us learn, as well as be a diversion. It isn't meant to let us hide from our problems instead of resolving them."

Pastel flushed, but to his great relief Zephyr switched topic. "This increase in timespacing will also benefit us Helpliners, though most of your colleagues won't see it that way. Thing is, as a department we've become complacent. You have inadvertently sent us scrambling, giving us our first genuine challenge since we set up shop. And for that I thank you. Rest assured, no one else will." Zephyr gave Pastel a gentle push. "Now, go relax until I call you."

And just how am I supposed to do that, Pastel wondered in the deepest part of his mind as he left. *Knowing I'll be facing a bunch of resentful colleagues I plan to betray?*

CHAPTER 9

"Boy, have you got pull all of a sudden!" Whisper marveled. "I'm right in the middle of a ticklish manipulation and my supervisor shoves me aside and says, 'Your buddy Pastel is free; go play.'"

Sirene appeared beside them, grinning. "Same here."

"I could get used to this," Murmur agreed, joining the group. She touched Pastel consolingly. "But rumor has it you won't be able to work on our island. Is that true?"

Despite the momentary thrill of contact with Murmur, Pastel felt his mood flatten. "Yes. I'll be getting very few breaks, and they'll be too short to do much more than recover. I think we'll also be spelling folks on the Helpline when we can."

"So? Who says you can't recover while you check on our progress? Maybe put in a suggestion or two?"

He brightened at that. "You're right. I was just feeling sorry for myself."

"Well, don't. You'll soon have a lovely island to return to." She was watching him closely.

So she thought the island project might keep him from leaving, Pastel realized. So, did she want him to stay, or not? "I guess this whole thing will take some getting used to," he said, noncommittally.

"Which 'thing'?" Sirene asked. "Being an instructor-in-training?"

"Or Entertainment Specialist Number One?", Whisper contributed.

Sirene turned toward Whisper with a bland expression. "Just who *is* this guy, anyway?"

"Oh, you know – some hotshot 'mover and shaker'."

Pastel's aura colored furiously. "Cut it out, you guys."

"Yes, cut him some slack, will you?" Murmur commanded, coming to Pastel's rescue. "He can't help being a celebrity and creative genius. Our hero has just been hiding it so us common folk wouldn't feel inferior."

"You're a *big* help!" Pastel pretended to bristle. "Maybe I'll just take my next break alone."

Murmur vibrated with mirth. "Sorry; I couldn't resist."

"Speaking of alone, was that your *Tree* I saw standing in the middle of nowhere?" Whisper turned to Murmur and imaged an oversized face with salivating mouth and eyes bugging out.

"As a matter of fact, it was. Did you want to book it? It'll be free a lot, now that Pastel has talked himself out of spending much time with us."

Pastel leaned forward and exuded mock belligerence. "You've got a mean streak. Has anyone told you that?"

"Just making sure you don't forget us 'little people'." Murmur imaged a wink.

"Since I'll be sweating it out with seven angry classmates – not likely."

Class is about to begin, Zephyr inserted into Pastel's mind.

Pastel gulped. "In fact, they're waiting for me now."

"I hope we didn't lay it on too thick." Murmur said, looking a tad guilty.

"Nothing my little ego can't handle," Pastel needled back before relocating to face the class. To his surprise, Solar Flare was absent.

Portions of him are outfocusing as an Orion and a Sagittarian, Zephyr informed

Pastel privately. *That plus his job was all he could manage.* "Alright, folks, let's get the introductions out of the way. During these courses, you'll get to know each other inside and out. Your strengths, weaknesses and eccentricities will become obvious to you and your colleagues. Don't try to hide them; they are part of who you are. If something would interfere with your training or effectiveness as an instructor, we will address it here in class. No fault-finding, no finger-pointing (so to speak). We just clear up the misunderstanding which holds it in place and go on from there. You will learn as much or more from the errors made and misperceptions brought to light as from what I teach you. *How* you learn is far less important than *that* you learn. Any questions before we begin?"

"Yes," a slight being piped up. "When do we get our mass upgrade?"

Now.

The area became suffused with brilliant energy. Everyone within its sphere of influence involuntarily leaned back from the intense power. The wave filled Pastel with a profound sense of quiet strength the likes of which he had never known. Then the energy source was gone.

Pastel transmitted to the unseen psyche a heartfelt 'thanks'.

You are quite welcome, the powerhouse replied, to Pastel's surprise. *Learn well.*

"Any *more* questions?" Zephyr asked drolly, then nodded at the absolute silence. "I thought not. Let's do the introductions and get to work."

Being the last to arrive, Pastel was at the far end of the semi-circle of occupied 'seats'. Deliberately, (or so Pastel thought), Zephyr started at the other end, gesturing at the first person to identify herself.

"Introspect. Helpline Team 4. Also a part-time designer of visual phenomena. Aurora borealis on Earth was my idea," she said with understandable pride.

The being next to her spoke up, mimicking the format begun by his team-mate. "Savoire Faire. Team 4. I don't have any formal hobbies, but I am constantly honing my social skills."

"Oh, admit it, Faire; you're a social butterfly," Introspect heckled.

Faire feigned offense. "I like people. What's wrong with that?"

"Next?" Zephyr interrupted the banter.

"Serendipity. Team 3. I had already put in for instructor training before this little 'crunch' came about." She flashed Pastel a humorous smile.

Well, at least that one won't ride my case, Pastel thought.

"Cold Fire," a familiar voice rumbled. "Team 2. I *had* just been approved to outfocus."

Pastel could see his aura bristle with hostility. *He should have called himself Cold Fury*, Pastel thought. *The way he holds a grudge.*

"Many of us have had to change our plans. And in some respects, that's a good thing." Zephyr surveyed the class as if daring anyone to contradict him. "The outfocused have to contend with the unexpected scuttling their plans; that's part of the challenge. Tell me: When was the last time any of you were inconvenienced here? Or challenged, for that matter?"

No one spoke, but Pastel could tell they were getting the message.

"Let's face facts," Zephyr continued. "Most of us are complacent egotists. We are immortal and omnipotent. Then along comes a 'Pastel', and suddenly we have to put our preferences on hold for a bit. How sad." Zephyr leaned forward to glare at his students. "You can get your plans back on track in an instant. All you have to do is get up and leave. No one will object or stop you."

After a momentary stunned silence, Fire started to rise. Then he thought better of it, and sat down again.

"Better now than later," Zephyr told him. "You're free to go."

This time Fire didn't hesitate. "No, I'll stay. But answer me one thing: What if this is just a fad, and people lose interest in timespacing once the island is built? We will have taken all this extra training for nothing."

"Really? What harm will it do you as a Helpliner? Or as a person, for that matter?" Zephyr shot back.

Fire shrugged. "None, I suppose."

"Next?"

"Whimsy. Team 3. I had been thinking of upgrading, but never quite got around to it until now." An easy twinkle followed that admission.

Both Sweet Memory and Silent Echo introduced themselves without comment, which left Pastel uncertain about their attitude.

"And lastly," Zephyr said. "The one person who needs no introduction: Cool Pastel."

That produced a few chuckles, and a snort of derision from Fire.

"Pastel has already had a refresher and one course. With your permission, I will transfer to each of you the salient details." As no one objected, Zephyr encapsulated the information and transmitted it directly into their minds. "Review it at your first opportunity."

"Pastel got to visit Earth. Can we, too?" The question came from Serendipity, who leaned forward eagerly.

Zephyr looked over at Pastel. "Which lesson stands out more in your mind? The one on Earth or the one in class?"

"On Earth, definitely."

"Why?"

That took a bit more thought. "Probably because there was so much sensory and emotional input. It felt *personal*."

"So be it."

"Thanks, boss." Pastel grinned, finding himself back in the same body Zephyr had assigned him before – or at least, an exact duplicate. They were in the same mall as before, but quite alone. A glance outside the closest window showed the reason: it was night-time.

Pastel was not surprised to see Whimsy, Memory, Serendipity and Introspect as attractive females, while Echo, Fire and Faire were handsome males. All except Zephyr were visually in their twenties. Zephyr was back in his wizard role, the white hair and beard making his apparent age indeterminate.

"I'll give you a few minutes to adjust to your surroundings – environmental as well as corporeal," Zephyr said. "But don't get too comfy; we won't be staying here."

Pastel wondered if their position next to a travel agency was deliberate. Enormous posters of pristine exotic locales, including several of tropic paradises, urged passersby to put themselves in the picture. Which, of course, reminded Pastel of both Zephyr's island and his own island project he'd no longer be able to participate in, other than vicariously.

It seemed mere seconds before their instructor was saying, "Ready?". Before anyone could reply, Zephyr made a minute gesture with his right hand, and the mall vanished.

Introspect was the first to recover her wits. "What are we doing in Spain?" she frowned. In her present embodiment, she had a very slight build complemented by long, straight, dark brown hair, brown eyes and finely-chiseled features. There was an air of nervous energy about her.

They were seated together in an outdoor stadium. On the field below, a bullfighter awaited the arrival of his quarry. Introspect wrinkled her fine nose in distaste. "I detest bullfights."

"We will be leaving shortly," Zephyr assured her. "Ah, here comes the bull."

The animal emerged from the dark bowels of the colosseum. Spears protruded from his back. Pastel winced, seeing the pain in its bovine eyes as it looked around for someone on which to vent its rage.

"Tell me," Zephyr spoke quietly to his students. "What is the attraction in this for the audience?"

"Danger," Faire said at once, leaning back against the stadium seat. His visual portrayal as a blond-haired, blue-eyed Adonis perfectly fit his obvious self-image. "The knowledge that one of them might be killed."

Zephyr nodded. "Danger."

Instantly, Pastel and his colleagues found themselves in the dimly-lit dining area of a soup kitchen. The style of the men's tattered clothing helped him place the era and location as the 'Dirty Thirties', probably in the American Midwest. A steaming cauldron of foul-smelling gruel rested on a rough-hewn table, and a ragged line of men curved out of sight through the doorway. One stocky individual, looking almost as disheveled as those in the chow line, stood on a narrow stage, yelling to be heard over the clatter of dishes and spoons.

Pastel and his group were in the far corner of the stage, which afforded them an unobstructed view of everyone in the room.

Zephyr addressed them in a normal tone of voice. "They cannot see or hear us. I want you to listen carefully to what the speaker is saying. I will question you on it afterwards. Not you, Pastel; stay out of this one."

Pastel nodded. He had already had the benefit of an extra course in time-space.

". . . give your hearts to the Almighty, and ye shall be free. I was once lost like you, but now I am found. I have seen the light; I have found The Way. Follow me down the righteous path, and ye shall be saved. So sayeth the Lord. Turn away from the evils of drink. Forsake the sins of the flesh . . .".

From what Pastel could tell, his words fell on deaf ears. Few bothered to look up from their meal and many, upon finishing, simply got up and left.

"Repent, all ye sinners," the preacher hollered at their departing backs. "Or ye shall suffer eternal damnation and forever burn in the fires of Hell."

"Heard enough?" Zephyr asked.

To a person, the students nodded. As Pastel had come to expect, that precipitated another change of venue. They stood beneath the overhang of a train station. It looked like the same era, probably the same drizzly evening.

"So here's the question: Of the two scenes you just witnessed, which is most dangerous to the human participant, and why?" Zephyr folded his arms and waited.

Echo – tall, lean and dark-skinned – was the first to speak. "On the surface, the bullfight. But in fact, the soup kitchen is."

"Why?"

"Because the handouts make them dependent."

Zephyr shook his head. "Right choice; wrong reason. When you're hungry, you'll go wherever there's food. This is only one stop for these men in an endless scrounge. The breadline is located close to the train station because these people are transients. They'll hop a train and hit another soup kitchen down the line, or they'll bum food from a promising-looking stranger, or from just about anywhere. They're drifters; they aren't dependent on any one person or place."

"Religion, then," Fire said. His shorter embodiment appeared to be of mixed Oriental descent. "They're in danger of getting hooked."

Zephyr lifted a bushy eyebrow. "How much interest did *you* see in that room?"

212

Fire shrugged a shoulder, conceding the point.

"But you're close. It wasn't the risk of being drawn *into* a particular philosophy, but of the timespacer being lured away from . . . ?" Zephyr paused, inviting them to finish the sentence.

There was a lengthy silence.

"From what they chose the lifetime to explore," Echo furnished at last.

Zephyr smiled. "Precisely. Remember: *Anything that would divert a person from what will provide the best learning and experience for his development and understanding is, in that sense, 'unsafe' for him.* That's right out of your Helpline manual. Based on that definition, without fully knowing the person and his goals (including those he 'landed' with), it is almost impossible to know what would be safe or unsafe for him.

As Helpliners, you're already familiar with the purposes the outfocused you are monitoring had for their excursion. But when a timespacer changes his itinerary on-site and you may not skip ahead and use foreknowledge to choose your input, you must then use that definition as your guide."

Red-headed freckled Whimsy scratched the side of her perky nose reflectively. "Most of the ones I monitor aren't that self-aware. They keep making the same mistakes over and over." She grimaced. "Sometimes, you know, I'd like to just stand in front of them and yell, 'For goodness sakes, look at what you're doing!'. I mean, we're talking real simple cause-and-effect stuff here."

"Simple for we who can see the 'big picture'," Zephyr stated. "But remember, we all did the same thing, repeating our mistakes endlessly when *we* outfocused.

Think of it this way: It's like spanking a newt for fighting with another newt. He doesn't know why he's being spanked, so he won't change his behavior. He'll just become confused and frightened and will mistrust you.

Many people fear life because they are being 'spanked' by it. They live in dread of the next spanking because they don't know what brought on the others. So they keep making the same mistakes. They don't realize these spankings result from living out limiting or damaging beliefs, behaviors and perspectives.

Those who are more aware have come to use the pats on the head and spankings in life as clues to which perspectives and beliefs are right or wrong for them. They in part share our overview of what is happening, and that's why they tend to progress faster."

Fire was frowning. "So? We learned all that in Basics."

Pastel was sure Zephyr would put Fire in his place, but if their instructor was annoyed he didn't show it.

"Learned it; yes. But as Whimsy's comment graphically illustrates, it is easy to forget that the purpose of many lifetimes *is* to experience that cause-and-effect and what happens when they get bogged down, internal-looping. Your callers, almost to a person, are ones exploring personal progress in a time-space environment. But the majority of excursions are *not* based on improvement. For them, improvement at the time-space level would be failure, specifically failure to fulfill the mandate they chose for the trip." Zephyr paused to ensure the students realized the importance of that fact. "If you encourage them to progress when their purpose is to explore some aspect of deterioration, *you* become 'unsafe' to them – a psychic saboteur. And some of you have come dangerously close of late."

Pastel swallowed convulsively. He sure wouldn't like to face a returning focus whose trip he had just ruined.

"I'm cold," Serendipity said, shivering.

The light drizzle had become a steady downpour and Pastel realized he, too, was feeling the chill.

"We're done here, anyway," Zephyr assured her.

This time, Pastel closed his eyes against the disorientation of being teleported. When he reopened them, they were standing on an airport runway with a jumbo jet bearing down on them at near-takeoff speed.

*

"GEEZ!" Pastel yelped. He crouched down and clapped his hands over his ears as the plane cleared them with a deafening roar. "What are you *doing*?"

"Reminding you all how real time-space can seem," Zephyr replied, as the engine's roar dopplered away. "And that's with us knowing the facts. Most timespacers don't have that advantage."

Whimsy shook her head sadly. "No, they don't. I keep forgetting that."

"Me, too," Fire admitted – somewhat reluctantly, Pastel thought. "But what are we here for?"

"To discuss death."

Pastel found his own surprise mirrored by his cohorts. Zephyr certainly enjoyed throwing them curve-balls.

"On a runway?" Echo's amusement gave way to suspicion. "Hey, wait a minute! We're not here to watch a crash, are we?"

"No. See that plane over there waiting for clearance?"

The jetliner in question was cueing up on *their* runway. Pastel fervently hoped they would not have to endure another overhead takeoff. His ears were still ringing from the last one.

"We're not going to *stay* here, are we, Zephyr?" Serendipity whined. She was Faire's counterpart in physical perfection, complete with the palest of blond hair and sea-green eyes.

"We will remain until we are done with this subject. So I suggest you pay close attention."

Pastel's eyes strayed to the massive machine. With an effort, he turned his attention back to what Zephyr was saying.

"As you know, humans perceive death as final, no matter how badly they wish to believe in what they call an 'afterlife'. That airplane can be used as an analogy for death."

Despite himself, Pastel felt his eyes being drawn towards the far end of the runway. The engines were revving up.

Zephyr raised his voice to be heard over the din. "Some of the people on that plane may be moving to a new country. Their experience will be much like leaving a lifetime. They will retain the memories of being here and what they experienced. They will have the 'not-here-anymore' perspective (objective, not immersed) and a whole new situation to interact with where they're going."

The jet started to roll, gaining speed with each passing second. Pastel couldn't take his eyes off it, but Zephyr merely switched to telepathic speech. Even so, Pastel realized belatedly that he had completely missed what Zephyr said.

Just as the plane was about to overfly their position, Zephyr relocated them to the lovely island which had so inspired Pastel.

"Thanks," Introspect said breathlessly, rising from a half-crouched position. She looked around her in surprise. "Say, this is nice."

Echo grinned. "Pastel's Island?"

Pastel sighed expansively, inhaling a lungful of air. "Home, sweet home." And froze. He risked a quick glance at Zephyr, but their instructor appeared not to have noticed the double meaning to his telling quip. "Actually, it's Zephyr's Island," Pastel amended quickly.

Ignoring the banter, Zephyr regarded them all pointedly. "Before you get too relaxed, answer me this, Faire: What were we just talking about?"

"What? Oh, something about death, I think." Faire glanced at the others for confirmation.

"What about death?"

" 'They're not here any more', wasn't it?" Pastel offered.

Memory nodded agreement. "Yes. And the plane figured in it somehow."

Fire started to chuckle. "I haven't the faintest idea," he admitted. "I don't believe it!" As his mirth gathered momentum, the others became infected. Pastel felt tears of laughter brim over, and their instructor's meaning solidly hit home.

"I've got to hand it to you, Zephyr, you got us good," Fire admitted, wiping his eyes.

Zephyr looked skeptical. "So the point of the lesson was . . .?"

"It's hard to think clearly with life barreling down on you."

"Well-enough put for a 'recess'. Here, or back home?"

"Here," chorused the class *en masse*.

"So be it." As before, a watch appeared on Pastel's wrist and, he presumed, on everyone else's. "See you at that flat rock yonder in one hour." With that, Zephyr walked away down the beach.

Faire enthusiastically rubbed his hands together. "So, Pastel, care to show us around?"

"Nope. You explore if you like. I want to swim."

Memory broke off from the group who were already heading inland. Long black hair down to her waist accentuated Memory's slim figure and Mediterranean features. "I'll join you."

After a moment's indecision, Echo and Whimsy turned back as well. They all disrobed before approaching the inviting aqua waters.

"It's not a large island. You'll have plenty of time to explore it," Pastel assured them. He glanced back to see if anyone else was coming, but the others were climbing the hill. All except Serendipity and Faire, that is. Those two were sneaking into a pocket of dense foliage, hand-in-hand.

Echo waded waist-deep before setting off on a brisk swim. Pastel and the others hurried to catch up. For several minutes, they swam in harmonious silence before rolling over to float in a leisurely fashion on their backs.

Memory sighed contentedly. "It may not be real, but this sure is living!"

"You said a mouthful," Whimsy agreed, languishing on top of the water. For some reason, she seemed more buoyant than the rest.

"About your island project: Have you figured a way for us to swim in our native form?" Echo asked Pastel.

"No. I'm hoping Zephyr will teach us."

Memory gave her head a little shake. "I suspect he has more practical matters in mind."

"Oh, I don't know," Pastel said. "As instructors, we'll need to create bodies to house our own students, when they're in our shoes. Maybe we can use the same technique natively." His intention to defect briefly impinged on his mind, but he resolutely pushed it back. That wouldn't be until his last course was over, anyway. In the meantime, he would learn all he could to help Murmur complete the island in nonspace.

Whimsy stretched out her arms and let her feet sink to the bottom. The water level came to just under her breasts, affording her male companions a provocative view. "Well, in case we can't, I intend to make full use of this body while I have it."

"I'll bet Serendipity and Faire are doing the same – but in a far more intimate way." Echo fluttered his eyebrows coquettishly.

So Pastel hadn't been the only one to notice. He let his feet find the ocean bed. "She couldn't get pregnant, could she? I mean, these bodies aren't *that* functional, right?"

Whimsy chewed her lip. "I don't know. But who would want in to a body that'll only be here a day or two?"

"I wouldn't put it past someone." Echo waded towards shore. "It might be a novel experience to be enclosed in a fully self-aware human being."

Memory looked at the others worriedly. "Should we warn them? Or tell Zephyr?"

"We don't even know for sure that's what they're up to," Pastel pointed out.

Whimsy sat down on the beach and hugged her knees. "They've been human enough times to know the risks. Besides, didn't we just get a lecture on interfering with other people's lessons? That goes for us immortals, too, you know."

Pastel nodded. Whimsy was right. Still, it could create a unique problem for Zephyr.

*

"I can't believe they actually okayed it," Murmur exclaimed. "And reassigned us to this project full-time. After all, it's just for entertainment."

Rocky, as the Terraformer referred to himself in the spirit of Helpline tradition, projected a philosophical smile. "I never question a gift; I just enjoy it."

The Aquarian, Waterboy, also took it in stride. "If it keeps the timespacing option in the forefront of people's minds, it'll serve a lot more purpose than just fun and games."

"It'll be a nice change to play in an environment we create, and remember we did so." The smaller of the Ecologists, Rubylith, produced a happy sigh.

Her mate, Open Arms, agreed, adding, "So, which do you think would be better? One humungous island? Or a bunch of smaller ones – maybe each quite different to cater to individual tastes and provide variety?"

Murmur chuckled. "I think you just answered your own question."

"I think I did, at that. What say you folks?"

Option 2 was the unanimous choice, so Murmur consulted her expansive nonspace allotment. "Rocky, should we make them close together, or spread far enough apart to not be 'visible' to embodied people?"

"I'd say the latter."

Arms projected a worried look. "Have you confirmed that you *can* embody yourself here?"

"Not yet. But Zephyr gave Pastel a human body during his first course. All we'd be providing is a spaceform version of one. That shouldn't be as hard."

"I don't know; I've never heard of it being done."

"Me either. If the instructors weren't so busy teaching, I'd ask one to train me." Murmur was silent for a bit. "Tell you what: You keep working on the islands, and I'll see what I can do about the embodiment angle."

Murmur transported herself under her Tree to think. Perhaps the library would hold something of use. Or she might catch an instructor between classes and beg a few pointers. Her confidence began to wane as Murmur considered her options. One thing was certain: If they could not come up with a way to encapsulate vacationers, the island project would literally be dead in the water.

*

"There's a *cave* over here!" Echo yelled in the distance. Pastel and the rest of his classmates quickly abandoned the sand castle they had been perfecting.

"Excellent!" Faire broke into a lope, towing Serendipity along. "I've always loved caves. Except for the time I was killed by a bear in one."

A few minutes later, they all joined Echo, having followed the sound of his voice.

"You know," Pastel realized as he gazed around the spacious cavern. "This looks a lot like the one I hid my loot in when I was a 15th-century pirate."

Whimsy shivered delicately. "I got lost in one once."

"Not much chance of that here," Pastel noted. "Zephyr would never let anything jeopardize his schedule. Right on cue, their wristwatches beeped, which eliciting a collective groan. Pastel glanced around, committing the topography to memory. "If we get another break, I can lead us right to it."

They had five minutes to get back on time.

"Who's game for a race?" Fire asked.

Turned out everyone was, so they took up positions in a straight line.

"Ready . . . set . . . *GO!*", Fire yelled.

Pastel ran along the shoreline, trying to get traction on the loose sand. Faire pulled up alongside, grinning wolfishly at Pastel before pouring on the speed. Pastel tried to close the gap which had suddenly grown between them, only to have Echo pass them both, reprising the Olympic sprinter techniques he had once embodied. The last of them – Whimsy – reached their instructor's location with two minutes to spare.

Zephyr regarded them quizzically. "In need of stimulation, are we?"

"No. Just got plenty of that," puffed Fire.

"Why did you do it?"

Fire gave a negligent shrug. "Because it's fun, of course."

With an expression of intense interest, Zephyr leaned forward to peer into Fire's sweaty face. "Was it challenging?"

"Yeah."

"So what you're saying is, it's fun to be challenged."

Fire looked at Zephyr, finally realizing he was being set up. "Uh, depends on the challenge, I suppose."

Zephyr cocked his head to one side. "What if someone were to offer you a *real* challenge? As a certain timespacer who was hunted to death on a similar island once told me, 'One man's fun is another man's challenge is another man's hell'."

Pastel tensed. He had an awful feeling something very bad was about to happen. Zephyr's eyes didn't look right, somehow. They shone with a strange light, and not for a moment did they leave Fire's face.

"Tell me, Fire, what would your 'hell' look like?" Zephyr asked conversationally.

The student swallowed, but did not reply.

"Like this, perhaps?" Zephyr's hand slowly extended to take in the entire island.

Pastel started to tremble. He risked a glance towards the hill. It was too far away for them to get to before one of those negligent flicks of Zephyr's hand could transport them wherever he wished, or keep them frozen in place, if he wanted to. They were at his mercy, and right now, he looked anything but merciful.

"Would you like to find out?" their instructor asked softly.

Fire shook his head, refusing to make eye contact.

"Why not? You just told me you like a challenge, and you obviously like to run." Zephyr stretched out that final word and smiled a horrible smile. "Would you like to run now, Fire?"

For an heart-stopping minute, nobody moved. Pastel felt as though he was rooted to the spot. When had Zephyr gone mad? Had he deliberately brought them here to hunt for sport? Pastel suddenly realized that this whole 'instructor training' gambit might have just been a ruse. What if Zephyr's preferred timespacing theme was as a mass murderer?

As all watched in horror, Zephyr stood up. He slowly raised his hand and pointed a forefinger at the group. "Gotcha."

Pastel gaped, unable to believe his ears.

"As I said, one man's fun is another man's challenge is another man's hell." Zephyr reminded them. "Look at you all; you're terrified. And of what? Did I ever threaten you in tone, language or action?"

Pastel replayed their tormenter's words in his mind. Zephyr was correct; he hadn't.

"Why?" Fire croaked. He took a step forward, fingers balled into fists. Pastel wouldn't have been surprised if Fire tried to kill Zephyr with his bare hands. "Why did you do that to us?"

Zephyr raised his eyebrows in mild rebuke. "To prove a point, of course. Several, actually. Every one of you took me for a maniac and believed that your lives were in danger. Despite the fact that 'you' cannot die, and that you *expect* me to dismiss the body you're attached to once the class is over."

Zephyr looked at each person in turn, and Pastel felt himself color. Caught again.

"Secondly, as you now realize, your reaction was based on a *perception* of danger. You interpreted everything I said according to that perception. And you would have based your actions on it as well, never revisiting the original event to consider the facts. And why?" Zephyr threw Fire's own question back at him. "*Because people seldom doubt their initial perception, whenever strong emotion is involved.*"

Whimsy sat down heavily, staring up at Zephyr. "Bloody hell!" she said in hushed tones.

Zephyr magnanimously accepted the change of topic. "Yes, let's talk about 'hell' for a moment. What did this bit of paradise become to you, when you thought you were stuck on it with an omnipotent lunatic – forgetting, I might add, that you are all omnipotent as well?"

Fire's mouth reluctantly formed a half-smile. "'Hell'," he admitted.

"Exactly. Perception again. When you indulged in your little foot-race, it was fun, right?"

Eight heads nodded.

"And a challenge?"

Again, all agreed that it had been.

Zephyr regarded them doubtfully. "Was it? What were you risking? What would have been the penalty for losing the race?"

"Nothing, really," Pastel answered for them.

"Then it wasn't a challenge. But when you thought you were in mortal danger, it became a challenge. In your perception, the penalty for losing the race was death. How much fun did you find it then?"

Memory shook her head forcefully. "None at all."

"Never forget, people," Zephyr shook a cautionary finger at them. "That most of the challenges the outfocused have so casually assigned themselves before they leave nonspace are no laughing matter to them once they're here and have forgotten they preordained it. It's so easy for us, as we lounge on the Helpline and dispense wisdom and perspective like a prescription, to criticize their often inept attempts to extricate themselves from their problems. But as you've just discovered – *again* – seeing the facts for what they are when you're caught up in something is no easy feat."

*

"Encapsulating yourself in a working spaceform body outside of time-space is no easy feat," Nebula was saying at the same moment. Murmur had corralled her during one of her brief respites to ask if such a thing was possible.

"But it can be done?"

"Yes. Although I've never tried it myself. I've had no reason to."

Murmur hesitated, reluctant to impose further on someone she barely knew and who obviously needed a 'breather'. But without the help . . .

"Any chance you could teach me? Preferably sometime soon, so we can put these islands to use?"

Nebula sighed tiredly. "I'll see what I can do. Let me get through this course first."

Murmur touched the instructor lightly in gratitude. Then, armed with a tentative agreement, she hurried over to tell the others they were in business.

*

"You know what really frosts my oysters?" Faire said unhappily as he looked down at his legs where they dangled over the rock ledge. "Everything you've taught us so far we already learned in Basics or from the manual. And yet, we all got suckered each time. I just don't get it."

The students were wedged closely together on the rock Pastel remembered from his previous visit. It had been spacious when there were just four of them, but now barely accommodated them all.

"The early parts *are* virtually the same," Zephyr admitted. "But in the Helpline course you learned the academics, the mechanics of it. Now you get to experience it first-hand. *Feelings* are involved. As Pastel noted, the experience is personal and that can make it downright traumatic. Not the sort of thing we can teach novices."

"Nooooo," Fire declared.

"But I can assure you, when we're finished you'll have a lot more patience with the timespacers you monitor, the novices you teach and the team you 'elder'. And that patience, also, will be personal, not just professional."

Pastel did not doubt it for a minute. He could almost regret that he wouldn't be putting it to use. Almost.

"Alright. I think you could use a rest from my voice – and my methods," Zephyr added with a grin. "Fire, I just put you through the wringer. Now I'll put you on the spot. While your colleagues go shake off the effects of my little jolt, you stay behind. You're going to teach the next lesson."

"Huh?" Fire looked startled.

Zephyr raised a restraining hand. "Don't panic. I'll describe the gist of it. You decide how you'll get the message across to that lot." His smile widened as all present turned suspicious eyes on Fire.

"You really are a sadist, you know that?" Fire looked like he meant it, too.

Zephyr's eyebrows raised. "What? You expected to become an instructor without ever teaching?"

"Well, no . . ."

Zephyr waved the rest away. "Scatter, folks. I don't want you anywhere near here. No peeking, no listening in. Go play. You'll be put to work soon enough."

With that veiled threat uppermost in his mind, Pastel followed the others down to the beach.

CHAPTER 10

"Why don't we go all the way and have a miniature sun and a moon or two?" Rocky suggested. "Part of what makes an island paradise so special are gorgeous sunsets and moonlight on the water."

"Very true," Murmur agreed. "But we don't have the expertise. And adding a time factor such as a setting sun could cause problems for some."

"Like Pastel, you mean."

"He's not the only one who gets caught up in time-space concepts." She considered the notion a minute before saying, "We could let people select night or day, and arrange to have a moon or sun in a fixed position."

Open Arms looked up from the pond bed. "Sounds good to me."

"But making a sun – that calls for a psyche," Rubylith pointed out. "And I doubt any of them would agree to do something that trivial."

But Murmur wasn't so sure. "*Someone* got us reassigned here, and who but the psyches have that much pull?"

"Why would a psyche care about – oh, of course: to lure folks in timespacing," Rubylith overruled her own objection. "Sneaky."

"I'll see if I can beg us a sun at least," Murmur decided.

"While you're at it," Rocky called after her as she moved away. "Get them to teach you to make bodies."

*

"I only did a quick review of your first course, but it didn't seem nearly as . . ." Serendipity cast about for the right word. "*Intense*. Do you think Zephyr's just trying to squeeze everything in quickly? Or does he think we're unusually dense and he's getting annoyed with us?"

"Definitely the former," Pastel assured her. "Zephyr trained me for the Helpline; I've known him for eons. He does what he must to get a point across, but that's as deep as it goes." He looked at his team-mates for backup, as they also had been trained by Zephyr.

"Pastel's right. It's just the tools of the job – ones we'd better learn, if we're to become effective teachers," Echo added.

"Damn! I've just been learning the lesson – well, reacting to it, mostly," Whimsy admitted. "I haven't paid attention to how it was presented."

"Me neither." Pastel could have kicked himself. Here he'd had a previous course, an extra opportunity to watch how Zephyr taught – and he'd blown it.

"So, what do you think Fire will do?" Introspect brought them back to the present. "Use shock treatment or not?"

Pastel had been wondering the same thing. In this class, Fire was the lone representative of Team 2. "Have any of you worked with him before?"

To a person, the others shook their heads. Which meant Fire was an unknown quantity, except for the brief stint he and Fire had shared. And, Pastel remembered, Fire had been the only one who took strong exception to being inconvenienced by taking this training.

Ready. The single word insinuated itself into Pastel's mind. The others looked at one another, silently confirming they, too, had heard the telepathic summons.

"That must be why Zephyr chose him," Faire said, as they started back. "None of us know what to expect."

So Zephyr's still keeping us off-balance, Pastel thought. He shook his arms and rolled his shoulders in an effort to relax suddenly-taut muscles.

As they approached the flat rock, Pastel looked around. Fire stood there, awaiting their arrival, but Zephyr was nowhere to be seen. Pastel wasn't the only one to notice, either.

"Oh-oh. What's Zephyr up to now?" Memory worried, shading her eyes with her hand for a better look.

Serendipity moaned. "I'm gonna be a nervous wreck if this keeps up."

Echo's dark eyebrows almost touched each other in a scowl. "Well, I don't know about the rest of you, but I'm tired of having my responses choreographed. No matter what happens, I'm not reacting."

"Overview the scene; that's the key," Pastel reminded them and himself. Echo was right; they were being much too predictable.

The group assembled in front of Fire, watching their new instructor warily.

Fire's eyebrows shot up. "Did I miss something?"

"Where's Zephyr?" Echo demanded.

Fire pretended to check his clothing, which they were all wearing again – presumably thanks to Zephyr. "Sorry. I seem to have misplaced him." Seeing the suspicion on everyone's face, he relented. "Look, guys. He told me what he wanted me to teach, then he just walked away. I haven't seen him since, and no, I *don't* know what he's up to. If anything. For all I know, he's just gone for a walk. He doesn't have to be here to monitor us, you know."

Which was true, Pastel realized, but it didn't make him feel any more secure.

Fire's tone turned conciliatory. "He's given me a job, and I'm allowed to do it my own way. So just let me do it, okay?" He looked at the faces still regarding him with open mistrust, and frowned. "I'll make you a deal: You do your best and don't hassle me, and I'll do the same for you when it's your turn. Fair enough?"

Pastel joined the others in tepid assent.

"Good." Fire expelled an exaggerated sigh. "And by the way, you'll like this one. I'm supposed to teach you to levitate."

Pastel felt his pulse quicken. "Really?"

"Levitate ourselves or an object?" Faire wanted to know. "Or both?"

"Any or all of the above. Told you you'd like it."

Echo looked skeptical. "Can *you* do it?"

Instead of answering, Fire closed his eyes, raised his arms from his side and, after a few moments' hesitation, gently lifted off the ground. He continued to rise until his feet were almost in line with Pastel's nose. "See? Nothing to it!"

"*Cool!*" Serendipity exclaimed.

Faire stepped forward eagerly. "Can you levitate me?" The words were barely out of his mouth before he, too, floated upward. "Alright!"

In seconds, Pastel and his companions joined Fire and Faire in midair. Pastel beamed. How many times, when he was embodied, had he dreamed of this moment, and finally he was doing it in the flesh.

"Now," Fire said with aplomb. "Your job is to get yourself down."

"What? How?" Echo asked in surprise.

"*You* figure it out," Fire smiled. "And remember, if you can lower yourself, you can raise yourself back up again. Just reverse it."

"It sounds so easy when you put it that way," Faire stated sarcastically.

Without moving a muscle, Fire turned around and floated back to the rock to watch.

"Never thought I'd be trying to *un*levitate myself," Pastel muttered. But if it was so easy that Fire could be taught in 15 minutes, surely they could get the knack of it on their own – at least, the getting-down part.

As he had seen Fire do, Pastel closed his eyes. He concentrated on what the sand would feel like under his feet. Then he opened one eye to peek. The beach was still five-and-a-half feet below him.

Alright; maybe you have to push *down*, Pastel thought, imagining a heavy weight pressing him toward the ground. But when he checked, he still had not budged at all. A quick glance at the others confirmed they had fared no better.

"Never thought a little gravity would be so welcome," Introspect said, grunting in effort.

Memory lifted a finger to garner their attention. "What if we try to jump *up*, then come down hard?"

Echo gave her a doubtful look. "I suppose it's worth a try."

Pastel attempted to spring upward, to no avail. Although his classmates made the same motions, they remained steadfastly in place.

"Obviously, manual effort isn't the answer," said the ever-practical Introspect.

Whimsy nodded. "Which leaves using our mind or feelings."

"Or both," Pastel said. "For most other things, using both at the same time works best." But nothing Pastel tried got him one inch closer to the surface.

Fire floated over in his surrealistic way, and stopped just outside their circle. "Give up?"

Pastel nodded sadly. "Unfortunately, yes." Once again, they had all failed the test.

"Alright, close your eyes. I'm going to transfer the instructions directly into your subconscious, like Zephyr did with me. You'll automatically be able to do it, then."

Pastel felt a slight tingling sensation in his brain. He waited for it to subside before opening his eyes. "Now what?" he asked.

"Now just decide what you want to do. But remember, you have to be *very* precise. That's the key with this stuff."

Once again, Pastel closed his eyes. This time, he spoke firmly inside his mind. *Lower the body down gently to stand upright on the sand.* That was as precise as he knew how to be.

"Excellent!" Pastel exclaimed, feeling the reassuring pressure of sand under his feet once more. He opened his eyes and watched his fellow students reach *terra firma* one by one. Not all landed squarely on their feet, though.

"Precise instructions, remember?" Fire told those who stumbled or toppled over.

"Bet *you* didn't do it perfectly the first time, either," Echo grumbled as he picked himself up and brushed off the sand.

But Fire had just begun. "Okay, now that you've gotten yourselves down, let's go back up together, in formation. On my mark. 1 . . . 2 . . . 3 . . . *NOW!*" Slowly, he began to rise.

Pastel hurried to catch up with him, slowing his ascent when he got abreast of their instructor's. The others were doing the same.

"Okay. Now rotate around in place. Like this:" Fire began to twirl slowly.

Amazingly, Pastel's body complied. All he had to do was decide on a particular maneuver and like magic, it would occur.

What a rush! Pastel beamed. He was keeping tabs on their leader as Fire came out of the spin to flat-glide.

"Now tip your body so it's horizontal to the ground," Fire instructed. "Lock in minimum and maximum height."

Obediently, Pastel selected 10 feet as his minimum, with a maximum of 80. It didn't take telepathy to know they were about to fly.

"Everyone done that?" Fire waited till he had gotten assurance from the group. "Okay. Spread out and practice. Keep a close eye on where the others are. We don't want any midair collisions."

"Now *this* is what I call a *lesson!*" Serendipity crowed as she spread her arms like a bird in flight. "I could get used to this."

Pastel let out a whoop of joy and peeled away from the pack to find his own space. *Streak* with *a body,* he exulted. *Wait till I tell my friends about* this!

He started off slowly, to get used to having mental control of his physical movements. Normally, in time-space, he was not fully aware of how the link between mind and body translated into automatic movement. And in his native state, there of course was no physical body to move – *unless you consider a ball of self-aware energy a physical body,* he thought, as he painstakingly performed a figure-8. But here it felt delicious to provide the mental direction and watch it be carried out flawlessly. Time fell away, as he gave himself over, body and soul, to joyous flight.

Pastel!

Mm?

Come back. The rest of the class is waiting, Fire transmitted, more bemused than anything.

Belatedly, Pastel realized Fire had been calling him. But the words had been so muted, merging with the sound of the wind in his ears, the surf swishing softly across the sand, the sea birds calling mournfully –

PASTEL!

Ow! Okay, I'm coming. Pastel wheeled around and tried to get his bearings. He had wandered farther afield than he had intended. Pouring on the speed, he shot across the sky toward their island, now over two miles away. Pastel had to swerve erratically once to avoid a small bird, but he made it back in surprisingly good time.

"Enjoy yourself?" Fire snickered, as Pastel landed at one side of the small gathering.

"Too much. I lost track of time. And space," he added, remembering how far he had gone. "Sorry."

"What about the rest of you?"

"Fantastic experience," Memory smiled happily.

Echo nodded. "Best I've ever had."

The others concurred, several voices speaking at once.

"Then perhaps," Fire said, his voice tinged with humor. "One of you would be good enough to teach me."

There was dead silence as his words sunk in.

Right on cue, Zephyr appeared beside Fire. "You handled that perfectly. I'll take it from here." He turned to face the others. "Fire doesn't know how to levitate. I've been moving him – and you at first – in concert with what he was saying." A little smile played at the corners of Zephyr's mouth. "His job was to convince you that he could levitate, so you would believe he could *subliminally* teach you how. That way, you wouldn't question the format. You would simply take it for granted that you knew how inside, and proceed on that premise."

"You underhanded –" Echo shook his head in admiration. "And *you* –" he shook a mock fist at Fire.

"Rise!" Zephyr roared at Pastel.

Pastel recoiled backward and upward in surprise. When he realized what Zephyr was doing, Pastel laughed self-consciously and lowered himself to the ground.

"Get the point?" Zephyr asked, looking around at a sea of grins and nods. "Besides teaching you a valuable skill, the crux of the lesson is this:

If someone believes in a lie, but can make it work to their benefit, it is a useful truth for them – at least for the moment."

He folded his arms across his chest. "Now, flock off while I prepare your last lesson. Pastel, you're the most skilled so far. Take Fire with you and teach him to fly."

As they turned to leave, Zephyr called them back. "While you're at it, think out your answer to this: How would you *succinctly* describe what you are, either natively or as a timespacer? Or, tell me how you would define time-space. I want your own thoughts; don't quote the manual or something you heard elsewhere. And don't discuss it among yourselves." Zephyr made shooing motions with his hands. "Okay, that's it. Go practice. And think."

Pastel peered over Faire's shoulder to locate Fire. The spurious levitator stepped forward, smiling blandly.

"I can't believe how easily you tricked us," Pastel marveled, as they walked down the now-vacant beach. The others had all taken flight. "Did you ever time-space as a con artist, by any chance?"

"Twice," was Fire's smug reply.

*

Murmur hesitated at the threshold of the psyche domain. Asking for a sun and moon had seemed so logical, but now it sounded foolish – a childish request. Yet without it, they would largely forfeit realism.

Murmur was about to turn away, then reconsidered. A psyche *had* sanctioned this project, after all. And since each knew everything the others did or said . . .

Still uncertain how her request would be received, Murmur mentally knocked. The transition was instantaneous. A being, itself resembling a small sun, approached.

"We have been expecting you," it said. "And yes, we will provide you with a programmable pseudo-sun and several moons to choose among."

"You will?"

"Your project will generate a significant increase in imagination and creativity, as well as generate increased interest in timespacing. To those ends, within reason, you have access to our resources."

"Thank you," Murmur exclaimed. "We will make our islands as inviting as we can." Without knowing how she knew,

Murmur realized that the interview was over. A moment later, she was outside their domain.

"It was so easy," Murmur told her crew, on returning to the project site. "I don't know why I always thought they were unapproachable."

"Anyone's approachable if you're doing what they want," Rocky cynically retorted. "My team once asked for more nonspace so we could spread out. We only got half of what we sought." He mentally reshaped a hill with such force that the rocklike base shifted and had to be reset. "It's not like there isn't endless amounts of the stuff."

Privately, Murmur wondered just how much they had wanted. Her SPS supervisor had toured the Terraformers' department once and commented that their work area was vast compared to that allotted to the SPS. Though, to be fair, Murmur could see that terraforming would require a lot more space.

"Did they teach you how to make pseudo-bodies?" Rubylith asked.

"Oh, no! How could I forget?" Murmur had been so delighted to be offered psyche resources that the question had completely slipped her mind. "But I don't dare go back; not yet. Let me try again on my own. Maybe I can figure it out."

Her colleagues were pointedly silent.

"I'm sorry." Murmur had goofed; what else could she say?

Rubylith projected a dollop of empathy which quickly morphed into mirth. "I probably would have done the same, faced with a psyche offering me the moon – moons even – and a sun, to boot."

Open Arms looked humorously aghast. "What? No stars?"

"I'm sure we can jury-rig something," Murmur rallied. One of Cindy the sage's maxims reminded her that they, too, were fallible:

Perfection is being the best you can be at that time and under those conditions.

"What do you think?" Rubylith asked, indicating the pond.

Murmur leaned over the edge to observe the waterlilies the Ecologist had been planting. They were set far enough from the waterfall to not be dislodged by the undertow. "Looks fine to me."

"When I let the water flow, I'll cut back on the volume coming over the falls if need be," Waterboy offered.

Rocky finished resetting and smoothing the hill. "Or I can change the lip-rock angles to spread the flow out over a larger area. By the way, Murmur, see all these indentations in the rocks? I made those especially for your plants."

"Wonderful," Murmur smiled. "And I have just the mosses to go there."

*

"But it's *easy,*" Pastel stressed, fighting his growing impatience. Try as he might, he couldn't seem to teach Fire to levitate.

Fire scowled darkly. "Well, if it's so darn easy, why can't I do it?"

"I don't know." Pastel wished he could just ask Zephyr to teach Fire himself, but knowing their instructor, Pastel was being tested as much as Fire was. And this time, Pastel did not intend to fail. "Unless . . ."

"Unless what?"

Pastel pursed his lips. "You made us think we could do it, and because of that, we were able to, right?"

"Yeah. So?"

"So, that gives me an idea." Pastel transmitted a cryptic message to Zephyr. A moment later, a blindfold appeared in Pastel's hand and droll approval entered his mind.

Fire's scowl darkened. "You've *got* to be kidding!"

"Nope. Follow me." Pastel favored his companion with a mock-innocent smile, delighting in the chance to turn the tables on the erstwhile scammer. He led the way to a small stand of palm trees near the foot of the hill. "Okay, turn around."

A snort of derision was Fire's reply.

"Oh, come on; don't be such a baby. I'm just doing my job, like you did. Now, keep still." Pastel tied the blindfold behind Fire's head, testing to make sure it wasn't too tight.

"Now what?"

"Now I levitate you a few feet." Which Pastel did, then tapped the under soles of Fire's sandals. "Fair enough?"

Fire was not impressed. "How does that help me learn to do it for myself?"

"Patience. Now, reach out your hands to touch the tree. Start feeling yourself rising, count to five, then lower yourself down again. Keep doing that. I'm going to help you and then, at some point, I'll let you do it on your own. Only you won't know when that is, if you're doing *your* job right," Pastel told him.

"We'll see."

"Okay, here we go. Think and *feel* going up about a foot." Pastel raised him slowly. "Your movement, with your hands against the tree, will let you see I'm not snowing you."

Up and down Pastel moved him, using a monotone and consistent rhythm. After a few minutes, Pastel felt a change in Fire's focus. Ever so slowly, Pastel eased back on the 'help'. There was no reduction in the movement. It took every bit of control Pastel had not to let his elation leak out.

"Now, let's go a little higher," Pastel said after a bit, still using a bored tone. "But not too fast, so your head doesn't touch the palms."

Fire increased his height by a foot-and-a-half.

"And stop." Pastel levitated himself so he could reach the blindfold and remove it. "There. You've been doing it by yourself for the last two minutes." Pastel raised a hand to forestall Fire's doubt. "Just do what you've been doing, and see for yourself."

Fire favored Pastel with a look of disbelief, then closed his eyes. Ever so slowly, he lowered himself until he was standing on the sand. "How do I know you're not still helping me?"

"I give you my word, you have been levitating on your own. So, do you want to get some practice in, or waste the time doubting me? We have an assignment to do, and I don't intend to face Zephyr empty-handed." Pastel turned and walked toward a patch of shade from which he could keep an eye on Fire.

By the time he sat down, his student was tentatively exploring level flight. Pastel watched the fledgling levitator until he was sure Fire could operate on his own. Only then did Pastel turn his mind to their assignment.

Something tapped his leg. Pastel jerked away, thinking it was a bug, but it was only Fire.

"You fell asleep," he accused. "I was showing off like mad, and you didn't even notice."

"Sorry." What Pastel was sorrier about was that he didn't have a definition ready. Or did he? An image floated in front of his mind's eye, and was followed by another and another. Pastel grinned, realizing what his subconscious was trying to tell him. It was elegant, almost brilliant. *I should nap more often*, he thought.

Return, please.

Fire nodded at Pastel, confirming he, too, had heard the summons. Since flying was faster and more enjoyable, they lifted off the beach and flew in tandem to join their instructor on 'Zephyr's Rock'. The others were flying in from all directions.

Zephyr grunted as they landed in front of him. "Never had a flock before." Turning his head toward Pastel, Zephyr rewarded him with a minuscule nod. "Good technique."

"Here's your blindfold back." Pastel presented the length of cloth to Zephyr with a flourish. The material vanished from his hand and, presumably, from time-space itself.

"Show-off," Fire snorted.

Zephyr ignored them both. "I gave you folks an assignment. Have you completed it?" Eight heads nodded. "Very well. Let's hear what you've got. Whimsy?"

She cleared her throat and closed her eyes as an 'aide memoire'. "*The more 'you' you are made up of here, the more alive you are. That's where your longevity comes from.*"

"Serendipity?"

"Mine's almost the same: *The more faithfully you express yourself in a play world, the more that world becomes faithful to you.*"

Zephyr merely nodded. "Next."

"I was thinking about what timespacers put themselves through. Here's what I came up with." Faire glanced around to make sure he had everyone's undivided attention. "*Any good game has windfalls and traps, prizes and penalties, puzzles and inventivenesses. That's why it's fun to play – because you go in with only your intelligence, awareness and a body you create as 'home base'.*"

Introspect was next. *"You are all-that-is-you attempting to express in three-dimensional thought."*

Pastel had to admit, that was succinct. His wasn't, but it tickled his fancy and he was chomping at the bit to recite it.

Fire prefaced his offering with "I chose time-space, but I didn't have much time to work on mine: *A time-space is a system of built-in limitations and resistances for a person to play within and ultimately overcome."*

"I chose who-we-are and am pretending I'm describing it to a caller," Memory said. *"I am the pattern your soul has when all your understanding and experience is merged into a single, self-aware energy being."*

"Echo?"

"I, too, worded it as though I'm talking to a caller: *You are a free-thinking, free-feeling, immortal, invulnerable thought-form piloting a three-dimensional body."*

Zephyr then turned toward Pastel with mild amusement. "So, did you *dream up* something for us?"

"I think that's about what I did do." Pastel grinned sheepishly. "I mean, it was in imagery and I had to translate it but, well, here goes. Oh, and it's also aimed at a caller:

Your lifetime is a deck you stack and restack and from which you deal yourself hand after hand. Make sure you stack the deck in your favor, and then have the self-thrust to play your hands to win. The game is living. The deck is the sum total of every experience you can have, based on your present Template. The hand you deal yourself is the next event you have drawn or projected yourself into. You, the player, are made up of your body, mind, feelings and spirit. Your wild cards are money and all other symbols of material worth to you.

Of course, I'm assuming the caller knows that his Template consists of his beliefs and truths, thoughts, perspectives, perceptions, attitudes, expectations, ethics, conscience, morality, and of course his feelings and emotions," Pastel added.

Zephyr permitted himself a brief smile. "Quite well done, all of you." He paused a full second to emphasize the compliment. "You may have noticed that, although every definition was accurate – and some more concise than others . . ." He flashed

Pastel a look of amusement. "You all perceive yourself, your Native Realm and the time-space environment differently. Your perception is as individual as a fingerprint. Which means your answers to timespacer questions will be unique." He regarded them pointedly.

Pastel furrowed his brow. "So how do we know the answers we're giving mesh with the caller we're giving it to?"

Zephyr pointed at him. "Good. Exactly. How *do* we know? Better yet, how do we *ensure* that the caller can understand and assimilate what we offer? Whimsy?"

"By being precise in our thinking, and speaking literally and lineally?"

"What if they're inferential learners? Literal doesn't work as well for them," Zephyr countered. "Don't just recite the first answer that comes to mind, people; *think* about it. I can wait." He crossed his arms across his chest and leaned back against the tree he seemed to have adopted as his own.

Pastel glanced at Echo and Fire, who were standing beside him, but they just shrugged.

"I guess bottom-line is that the callers must be able to *feel* what we're describing; it has to come to life for them. Otherwise, they won't bother with it," Pastel stated. No matter what Zephyr said, that element was crucial.

"Yes. Very important. But that's only half of the equation. If you put it right, they'll feel and accept the perspective – hopefully after critiquing it and before trying to apply it. They mustn't just accept anything, including input from us, at face value. But they apply it based on what, Faire?"

Pastel watched understanding dawn on everyone's face. It was so obvious, when Zephyr put it that way.

"Their perceptions," Faire replied, for the record.

"Their *Template*," Zephyr corrected. "They run it by their beliefs and biases and view it from within whatever their mood is; the list goes on. How similar to what you transmitted is it likely to be, once it's gone through all those filters?"

"Ouch," Pastel said softly.

"That's why it is so important that you, or one of your team-mates, follow up.

Sure, you answer their questions and give them advice. But how many of you *ask* questions of your own?" Zephyr looked from face to face. "No? Why not?"

For the life of him, Pastel couldn't think of a good reason. Nor, apparently, could anyone else.

Their instructor didn't seem surprised. "Communication goes both ways. Your homework is to use what you learn in these courses. Use them on the Helpline, and with your friends and colleagues. *Listen* to what others say, how they view things, and how their perceptions influence their decisions and actions. Ready to go home?"

Pastel looked longingly at the ocean, inviting and so close.

"Um . . ." Serendipity began.

Zephyr sighed. "Oh, alright. One hour."

The ubiquitous watch sprouted on each recruit's wrist.

"Off you go."

Pastel didn't have to be told twice. To a person, they lifted off and zoomed toward whatever diversion drew them the most.

CHAPTER 11

While the others prepared new sites for her plant-forms, Murmur resolutely strove to create a pseudo-body she could occupy. Making the body was easy. Getting inside and being able to mobilize it from within was a different story. So far, nothing she tried worked. The 'body' just stood there motionless.

"I give up," Murmur groaned at last. "I just can't do it."

Waterboy looked down from the ledge on which he was perched. He was carefully threading a pristine spring through the hillock.

"Why don't you try it the other way around? Encase yourself in a skin. Wrap it around you."

"That's an idea."

Murmur carefully extended herself in various directions, until limbs, a female torso and a head had taken shape. She regarded her reflection in the water. "Does this look right to you?"

The Aquarian surveyed the effect. "The arms and legs are too long for the body. And the head is sort of off-center."

"Yes. I see what you mean." Murmur made the necessary adjustments, then added fingers, toes and facial features. "How's this?"

"Much better."

Rocky emerged from a ground-level cave he was carving. "Hey, that's pretty good!"

"Thanks. But it won't help me much if I can't build a skin of some sort to house me."

"Maybe you don't have to. See if you can 'walk' on the beach, and then try swimming. Waterboy, is the pond ready yet?"

"My portion is. But check with the Ecologists first. I don't know if the water lilies are rooted well enough."

Arms was closest. Murmur transmitted the query to him.

They'll hold, he assured her.

The sand tickled her 'toes', but lacking weight, Murmur didn't make any headway. Too little of her essence was touching the surface, and what was in contact made no impression in the sand.

Maybe if I scrunch more of myself into my feet, Murmur thought. She widened, thickened and elongated them to provide better traction. By mentally pushing herself down, Murmur found she could now move forward, even though it was more like a light surface bounce. She discovered there was a lot to keep in mind which would have been automatic in a time-space body. Murmur practiced walking up and down the newly-completed stretch of beach for a while, but it still didn't feel quite right.

"Not bad," Rubylith remarked. She was planting bulrushes along one edge of the pond. "Have you tried swimming yet?"

Murmur shook her head. "No, I'm just about to." She veered toward the pool, then balanced on one foot while she touched the surface of the water with a toe.

"Is the temperature alright?" Waterboy asked.

"Perfect. Well, here goes." With one hand, Murmur grabbed a vine she had arranged for just that purpose. But the cord effortlessly severed the bit of essence she had devoted to fingers. Murmur had to corral the errant portions and herd them back into place.

"Why don't you just hover above the water and drop into it?" Rocky suggested.

Murmur regarded the pool doubtfully. It suddenly looked a lot less inviting. "I might go 'splat' and break into dozens of pieces. No, I think I'll just lower myself."

Horizontal and face down, Murmur eased herself onto the pond. She floated on top like a leaf. Try as she might, Murmur could not breach the water with her essence and, remembering how easily the vine had severed her fingers, she dared not try to plunge her hands into the water by force.

With a sigh of defeat, Murmur projected herself back onto the beach and assumed her normal shape.

*

"*There* you are!" Pastel exclaimed, as he appeared next to Murmur. Was it wishful thinking or did she look especially happy to see him?

Murmur turned towards Pastel, having just nudged aside a pond plant leaf that was throwing unwanted shade on one of her aquaflowers. "Perfect timing. I need your advice. But first, how did your course go?"

"Unbelievable! There's so much I want to tell you." Pastel gaze wandered and was immediately snared by the waterfall and various other points of interest on the burgeoning island. "Wow! Speaking of the unbelievable . . ."

Murmur projected a self-deprecating smile, but Pastel could tell she was pleased. "Yeah, it's coming along fine. But then, I have a lot of help." Murmur nodded toward her workmates who were popping up like so many gophers to see who had arrived.

Spying Pastel, the Terraformer barged ahead of the others. "Man, you sure had a great idea here." He gave the Helpliner a friendly shove. "Well? What do ya think? Is that what you had in mind?" He fairly oozed satisfaction.

Pastel stared at him, taken aback. "Say, aren't you —?"

"Yup," he interrupted smugly. "Call me Rocky. I wangled the job for myself. Had to promise to work extra shifts, but . . .". He gestured towards the hill behind them. "I think was worth it."

As Pastel drank in the details, his amazement grew. "You can say that again, several times over! I can't believe this."

Rubylith insinuated herself between Rocky and Pastel, nudging the Terraformer back with an impudent grin. "Hey, share, will you?" She turned to Pastel with a Cheshire-cat smile in her mind. "I'm Rubylith and this is my mate, Open Arms. We're your Ecologists. I know you and Murmur decided against having fauna, but it wouldn't take much to make pseudo-trout and bass if you think folks'd like to do some fishing. And I'm sure Rocky here could conjure up a few suitable spots to fish from. Or maybe we could enlarge the pond a bit."

Pastel glanced at Murmur for her opinion, but Arms interjected, "Or I could make another pond – maybe even a small lake – just for fishing and maybe boating. Oh, I wonder if we could water-ski too? I used to love that." His mind trailed off into reminiscences, then he asked, almost as an afterthought, "Should we have seasons? Lots of people like snow sports."

"You're bringing up all sorts of things I never even considered," Pastel said. "And they're all great ideas. But wouldn't that take a lot more space? I don't know how much we can have."

"All we want, the psyches said," the last member of their team stated by way of introduction. "By the way, I'm Waterboy, your Aquarian."

"*ALL* we want?" Pastel's mind boggled. He'd never heard of the psyches giving *anyone* that kind of latitude, ever.

Murmur laughed. "Pastel, maybe we'd better go someplace quiet, and let these folks get back to work. Looks like we have a lot to discuss, and I have a little problem you might be able to help me with."

*

The psyches convened a meeting within their merged minds, as psyches were wont to do. Among themselves, they of course thought in the accurate, tenseless language of 'now'.

The progression Pastel sets in motion branches out in unanticipated directions, psyche1 observed. *Its soulmate attempts to introduce its native essence into the time-space element, water.*

271

*And to encapsulate its essence inside –
and drive – a human-like body*, psyche4
added. *It is wise of you to suppress its
memory of wishing to ask you how.*

Psyche2 agreed, adding, *the benefits of
it learning on its own, or in concert with its
companions, are too great to squander.*

Pastel's tutor also impresses, stated
psyche1. *Not only are its methods highly
innovative, but it is instilling its own
unpredictability into its students. We note
in particular the two methods of teaching
levitation.*

Psyche3 said, *The common element is
Pastel. It is what the human timespacers
call the 'wild card'. Let us not forget, it is
also Pastel which urges Earth Helpliners
to act human and adopt their amusing
pseudonyms. I believe that is where the
advancement begins.*

*Without it realizing the facts, Pastel's
talent for stimulating change must be
nurtured and protected at all costs*,
psyche4 declared. *That is, if it does not
forsake reality.*

Psyche1 let its dubiousness be felt.
*Pastel's strongest urge is for love and
approval. Despite enjoying unprecedented*

popularity, it remains unaware it is loved.
The psyche left the inference open.

Then we await its decision, psyche2
ruled.

*

"Amazing, isn't it?" Murmur sat beside
Pastel under their Tree. "The changes that
are going on around here? I've never seen
so much enthusiasm and activity."

Pastel produced a happy sigh. He was
feeling decidedly mellow. "It's downright
refreshing."

"Indeed. It's like we're on vacation –
but here." Murmur turned to look at Pastel.
"You know, I just realized something. We
all have our career of choice and our
hobbies and socializing between work
shifts, and all. But except for the portions
of ourselves we outfocus, we don't have
vacations."

"And timespacing is often anything
but," Pastel stated. "No wonder our island
concept is so popular. We can finally have
real vacations here at home."

We? . . . home? That brought him up
short. It sounded like he intended to stay,

when in fact he didn't. Careful to shield his thoughts from Murmur, Pastel revisited the reasons he could not remain. A lot of changes were occurring both here and in his personal life, but they were transient, he reminded himself. Once the island was complete, Pastel would again sink into anonymity, Murmur would return to her SPS project, and the two of them would quickly fall back into their old, untenable rut. If Pastel stayed, he'd spend eternity without love. That was the bottom line, and that was the one thing he could not face. But in the meantime, he would enjoy to the fullest these precious moments with Murmur.

*

"You wanted to see me?" Zephyr asked the psyche who met him inside the portal.

"Indeed we do. We wish to discuss with you your teaching methods."

Zephyr hesitated. Were they objecting or . . .

"We are not," the psyche stated firmly. "They produce remarkable results. It is our recommendation that, once the current rush

274

subsides, you extend it as an upgrade for all seasoned Helpliners. Of course, you must tailor it to the temperaments of your students. Not all would adequately tolerate your unconventional shocks." That comment was laced with humor.

Zephyr nodded. "I wasn't certain these would, either. But they are unusually resilient, and extremely bright. Although I wouldn't want that to get back to them, if you know what I mean."

"We do. And we encourage you to draw out the unorthodox natures of your students by whatever means you can. The results so far are most impressive." The psyche inclined its upper surface just enough to indicate appreciation. "We will not keep you from your well-earned 'time off'."

Zephyr found himself back outside the threshold. Smiling inwardly, he went in search of privacy.

*

"How're you doing, buddy?" Whisper greeted Pastel, with a broad grin for Murmur.

"Great. How about you two?"

Sirene slunk up against Whisper. "That depends. Is the Tree available?"

"Sure," Murmur said easily. She and Pastel had just finished their meeting and the verbal exchange of recent experiences. Murmur had never felt so close to Pastel. It had taken all her self-control to keep her true feelings for him from leaking out.

Whisper was surveying his mate with mock exasperation. "Is that all you ever think about? Here we have my bestest buddy, freshly returned from the trenches – picture war wounds here and here." He prodded Pastel impudently in two places. "And all you can think of is –"

"Shaddap!" Sirene laughed, shoving Whisper unceremoniously towards the Tree. As a grinning Whisper disappeared behind the hairy fronds, Sirene transmitted a private message to Pastel and Murmur. *Whisper won't admit it, but his ego is taking a beating.*

Why? Pastel tight-banded his surprise.

How would you feel if your closest friend suddenly became the toast of nonspace, and all your co-workers want to talk to you about is 'pulling strings' with your buddy? Not to mention us being 'let out' whenever you show up, so we can keep you entertained. Don't get me wrong; I don't mind a bit. But Whisper is more sensitive than me.

Pastel glanced at Murmur in dismay. *I'm so sorry*, he replied mentally. *I didn't know. When you're free, please tell me how I can help.*

I will. Sirene's feelings abruptly became highly sensual, so Pastel hastily withdrew.

Murmur gestured toward an unoccupied section of void nearby. "Follow me." Once they had relocated, she rounded on Pastel. "You stop that right now!"

Pastel recoiled from her unaccustomed fierceness. "Stop what?"

"The shame you're feeling. You have no reason to feel guilty. Well, not about that, anyway," she corrected herself. "This project of yours will be wonderful for everyone. If Whisper's ego gets bruised a bit in the process, too bad; he'll survive."

Pastel regarded her in astonishment. "But he's my friend. The last thing I want to do is hurt him." And the time when he'd be doing just that was fast approaching. The thought made him feel even worse.

Murmur regarded him silently for a moment, then decided to try a different approach. "Whisper has always been a step above you, career-wise, right?"

Pastel nodded, his expression guarded. Murmur could see that, deep inside, the disparity rankled him.

"But you didn't feel inferior."

"Well, yes, but I never let on."

Murmur softened her stand a bit. "My point is, you're special, Pastel. I don't know how or why, but you are. When you are around, things happen, things change – sometimes even for the better." She gave him a ghost of a smile. "Whisper will get used to the reflected glory –"

"Murmur!" It came out almost as a wail. Pastel quickly tempered his mental output, but the outburst had been telling. *"Anyway, it's got nothing to do with me any more. You and your crew are doing all the work."*

She managed a physical shrug. "It's a moot point. As soon as those islands are finished, people will be too busy enjoying them to care how they got there."

Pastel stared at her. "Islands plural? When did that happen?"

"When it became *the* place to be – sight unseen and unfinished. You don't *know* how many inquiries we've had! The sooner we get them finished, the sooner we'll stop being pestered."

"How soon do you figure that'll be?"

"At the rate we're going, not long." Murmur opened her mind to Pastel, as it was the quickest way to fill in the blanks. "But that's not the real problem. It's how to interact with those environments." Murmur described at length her attempts and the disappointing results. "Somehow, we have to envelop ourselves in a strong but pliable 'skin' and amass weight. Only I don't know how, and I'd rather not ask the psyches for help again. This is *our* project; I want to keep it that way."

"Hmm . . . in our course, we learned to levitate ourselves while in human bodies. Wouldn't the opposite of that be to become heavier?"

"It might be."

Pastel nodded towards the island in the distance. "I've an idea."

*

They appeared on the island in virtually the same spot they had left. The rest of the team had now completed the entire front of the hill, and had added aesthetic touches to the waterfall and pond. A host of exotic flowers framed the terraced levels of the hillside where the waterfall flowed in a white velvet cascading sheet. Portions of the rock face were extended in gently-cupped wide ledges filled with thick, soft mosses. Pastel knew those ledges would make popular bowers and perches.

"What do you think?" Rocky came towards them, beaming proudly. "Notice the ledges?"

"Sure did! What a great idea! But who planted the flowers?" Pastel asked.

"I did." From behind an enormous palm tree, an SPS emerged. "Call me 'Rose'," she giggled.

"How wonderful! I was hoping you would give us a hand." Murmur rubbed her colleague's aura affectionately. "It's stunning. Oh, um, *Rose*, may I present the person whose mind child this was: Cool Pastel."

"Ever so glad to meet you," Rose's smile was as bright as any sun. "I hoped you'd come by. Is that what you had in mind?" She motioned towards the flora.

"No, but I wish it had been. They are breathtaking."

Murmur nudged him gently. "You had an idea?"

"Oh, yes. I was thinking maybe for the walking part, all you need is a bit of weight."

Murmur projected a raised eyebrow. "You want me to walk around carrying a rock?"

"No. Hang on a minute; I want to try something." Remembering the sensation of weightlessness he had achieved while embodied, Pastel reversed the mental instructions until he felt the sand press firmly against the under-portion of his aura. Then he locked in that level of pressure.

"You're leaving a solid indentation in the sand," Murmur confirmed. "But can you do so with 'feet'?"

"Let's find out."

Having so recently enjoyed human form, Pastel found he could effortlessly rearrange his essence. Now for the real test. He verified that the weight was sufficient to the task, then walked the length of the beach. But when he broke into a trot, the undue pressure on his toes caused them to flatten out, and a few even separated from the rest of his essence.

"Oops." Pastel corralled the bits back and reassimilated them. "I see what you mean. We probably will have to form a 'skin' around ourselves. Unfortunately, I don't know how to do that – at least, not yet."

Murmur morphed a conciliatory smile. "Well, we needed the weight part, anyway, so perhaps you could show me how to do that, for now."

"Why certainly, my dear." Pastel bowed gallantly, and proceeded to teach her the mechanics of having 'weighty thoughts'.

*

"So *this* is what all the hoopla is about!" Sirene exclaimed some time later, having just teleported herself onto the beach.

Whisper appeared alongside her to say "Wow! No wonder people are anxious to come here. When'll it be finished, Pastel?"

The Helpliner shrugged eloquently, now that he had shoulders with which to do so. "Don't ask me; it's their project."

In a twinkling, Pastel was forgotten. Bemused, he watched as his friends gave Murmur and her crew the 'third degree', interspersed with a growing wish list of amenities. At least this time Pastel felt no jealousy, he noted with satisfaction.

Shift beginning. Pastel recognized the mindprint of Echo.

"Sorry, folks," Pastel interjected as soon as he could garner their attention. "Duty calls. Catch you later."

*

"How's the island coming?" Memory asked as soon as Pastel was 'seated' at the Helpline.

"It's extraordinary. And it's only the first one. They're making a whole series of them, all different. There'll even be a sun and an assortment of moons for each, I understand." Pastel still found it incredible that his little idea was being transformed into something so immense and realistic.

"Ooh! I can hardly wait." Moments later, Memory signaled that someone was calling in.

Pastel mentally adjusted himself to monitor the call as well as his own presently-idle frequency.

Pay special attention to your callers' perceptions and notice the effects those perceptions have on their lives, Zephyr transmitted to the Team 1 members who had attended his course.

"It's Hide and Seek, aka Takka and Juneth, the 12-year-old, 28th-century twins on Europa," Memory told Pastel quickly before opening up to the callers. The twins were fully telepathic to each other and always used a mind-merge when they contacted the Helpline.

"We got our hands on an old 23rd-century hol-image book from *Earth*," Juneth began, making it sound like the remarkable feat that it was. "It talks about 'reality' – people sure had some strange ideas back then, didn't they?" Juneth commented to Takka in mid-sentence.

"Tricksome," Takka agreed.

"– and 'what is real' like they are two different things. We've been discussing it

284

and we agree, but we don't know what the difference is –" Juneth explained.

"– but we figured you would know. Do you?" Takka got to their question at last.

Memory smothered a grin. "Yes, and you're right. 'Reality' and 'what is real' aren't always the same. For example, a shadow doesn't exist as a real item, but you can see it and there is a measurable temperature drop in a shadowed area. So it's part of reality but it isn't 'real', in that sense. Also –."

"Don't forget to ask about emotions," Juneth said in an aside to Takka, interrupting Memory in her urgency.

"I won't." Takka turned her attention back to the Helpliner. "That book also said, *'Think of yourself as a three-sided pyramid: mental, physical and feelings/ emotions. Deny any one and the structure cannot grow evenly. Deny it too long and the structure will fall.'* Is that true?" Takka's mental voice took on an apprehensive edge.

Pastel knew which of the three elements had them worried. Emotional expression was frowned on in their society.

Pastel and Memory shared a private smile, for both recognized the quote as belonging to Safe Haven from his lifetime as Peter, the Austrian therapist. Though the statement had been meant primarily as a self-warning, for Peter often denied himself the emotional and feelinged outlets he helped his clients attain, the caution had somehow made it into a hol-book.

"Yes, it can be true," Memory admitted. "Each has its own purpose in your make-up. Each lets you experience your world and express yourself in it. Not using one of them would be like –" Pastel felt his colleague cast about for a suitable analogy. "– you two not speaking telepathically."

Pastel heard the twins gasp.

"That would be *monstrous!*", Juneth squealed. "I could *never* live that way!"

"It's just an example, dimp," Takka chided her sister. Then to Memory: "We don't hide our emotions from each other, just from people. That's okay, then, isn't it?"

Memory projected a calm reassurance. "Yes. As long as *you* continue to feel, it doesn't matter whether you let others see it or not."

"That's a relief," two mental voices said almost in unison before they disconnected.

"Delightful personas," Memory said. "It'll be fun to watch them set that oh-so-deliberate culture on its heels."

"And get away with it," Pastel added. "Most societal innovators use the backlash as their exit. I was glad that they plan on sticking around to direct it."

A niggling sensation steered Pastel's focus to his own frequency. Clarity, aka Aria, the Shawnikan colonist was calling in, her tone rich with excitement.

"She *reached* me!" Aria announced as soon as contact was established. "Bruth, the leader of the Orion attack force that was going to wipe out our colony. We actually *talked* – in images, of course. It was the most amazing thing. And she's coming here alone, to meet me in private."

Pastel projected warm approval. "Our congratulations."

"Thanks. She promised I'd be safe and that they won't harm us or take us over or anything, and I believe her," Aria said breathlessly, still overwhelmed by her unexpected success. "I'd love to introduce her to our Administrator, Jeremy, but I think it's too soon for that."

Pastel had to agree. "Since no one knows you've been in touch with her, it might be wiser to keep it to yourself for now."

"If only we could talk normally." Aria's 'voice' turned wistful. "It's so awkward using images."

From what little Flare had said about Bruth, Pastel suspected in time they would overcome that obstacle. They might even become friends, now that they could communicate telepathically. A wisp of memory tickled the back of his mind, but he couldn't grasp it.

"Maybe I could teach her enough of our language or learn enough of hers to get by," Aria continued. "But I just wanted to tell you what happened, in case you didn't know."

"Thank you," Pastel replied.

When Aria left, Pastel consulted Zephyr who, as usual, was monitoring the shift. The recollection had fallen into place.

"Could Aria and Bruth become soulmates there?" Pastel let the statement hang by way of query.

Zephyr nodded. "It's certainly possible. Soulmates often meet in time-space long before they combine here. And even those who are mates here often give themselves challenges in time-space to see if they can recognize each other under unconventional circumstances. We've seen war enemies, same genders, mentally disabled, different races or species, and all sorts of other combinations give it a try, and they often succeed."

At that moment, Zephyr's frequency was activated. The caller was Peter, whose quote had just come up in Memory's conversation with Hide and Seek.

"I know we choose lifetimes to explore certain things, but I was wondering, is there one main purpose for timespacing?"

"There is," Zephyr replied. "Earth is as alien a realm as you can imagine, but you consider it home. The environment of thought, energy and consciousness is your permanent residence, of course. But to you, immersed in time-space as you are, your native realm seems invisible and nebulous.

Eventually, after you have lived a great many lifetimes, you will no longer be able to blot out awareness of who you are and where you come from. By then, you will have developed your selfhood expression to the point where you recognize yourself, no matter what environment you place yourself in."

Pastel felt as though he'd been jabbed with a cattle prod, but Zephyr continued on, apparently oblivious to the blindside he had just delivered to Pastel.

"The primary goal of having lifetimes, Peter, is for the awareness of your true selfhood to become so strong that it outshines, overpowers or overrules all obstacles it comes up against in any environment. It must be able to do so no matter how little energy and consciousness you have projected into that environment to play out the part. *That* is the point of being whole, and being whole is the crux of being."

"Thank you." Peter disconnected a moment later.

Pastel stared at Zephyr in horror. He craved the merciful amnesia of time-space. But if he moved all of himself there, *what if he couldn't forget*? The thought was so terrifying that he almost missed Echo's imaged wave to get his attention. It took a moment of concerted effort, but Pastel managed to dampen his reaction enough to follow the conversation.

It was Open Mind, aka Ricky, the recovering alcoholic.

"Hello, Ricky," Echo said.

"Uh, hi. I just wanted to tell ya I got me a job. It ain't much – just sweepin' floors an' stockin' shelves, but it oughta keep me fed and get me a room of my own somewheres."

Echo projected warmth. "That *is* an excellent start."

"An' I was thinkin', maybe I could get a book or two. I used to like readin'. Maybe even somethin' educational."

It was obvious to Pastel that Ricky was using the Helpliner as a sounding board. He transmitted to Echo, *He's in planning mode.*

I know. "I believe you enjoyed writing, too, when you were in grammar school. Remember the short story your teacher loved?"

Ricky groaned. "That silly thin'." But he was smiling at the memory.

"Why? Think you could do better now?"

Pastel felt the instant change in Ricky. He sat upright on his cot, as half-formed thoughts and old feelings flooded back. "I dunno." There was a pause, as snippets of that story resurfaced. "Maybe I could."

"We think you could, too. You might want to choose some books that are popular now, of the type you like to read. See if they give you ideas." Echo was carefully planting a seed which, if it germinated, would give Ricky something to focus on other than avoiding a bottle.

"Yeah. Maybe I will. Gotta go. Bye."

Pastel wished he could peek in on Ricky a few years later, to see if he had written anything. But this was now an 'improv' lifetime and previewing was banned. That was something else Pastel would miss, seeing how certain lifetimes turned out.

A familiar niggling sensation returned his focus to his 'line'.

"Hi, Pastel, remember me?" an impish 'voice' asked. It was surprisingly strong, considering the body to which it was attached was terminating.

"Peaches?"

"*And* Cream," Martha, the dying senior Pastel had met in the hospice assured him. "George slipped into a coma this morning. I wanted to reach you before we leave, to thank you for coming in. I can't tell you how heartening it was for us to know – to have *confirmation* – that we'll be together always. See you soon."

"Well, technically, you know, neither of you actually left. You just projected a small bit of your focus and energy . . ." Pastel stopped, realizing that between one word and the next, Peaches, aka Martha, had returned home.

Soon, an indulgently-grinning Peaches appeared before Pastel, the timespacing energy/focus having reintegrated with the rest of her essence. "Sorry. I kind of cut you off there."

Pastel reached out to touch his radiantly alive colleague. "No problem. It was a treat to meet you 'in the flesh' – what little there was left."

"I *was* a sight, wasn't I?" Peaches flexed her deliciously-responsive aura. "It's always great to get back, and I must say, that was one of the nicest trips I've taken, but —". Peaches favored Pastel with a look of reproach. "Where are the peaches and cream you promised us? Not that we could eat them, of course, but a deal's a deal."

"Not till Cream gets here," Pastel wagged his best impression of a forefinger.

"Ahah! Here he comes now. Talk about timing! On second thought, we'll be back later for our 'just desserts'."

Pastel produced a lecherous grin. "Much later, I'll bet."

"Much, *much* later." Peaches vanished with a flourish.

There were no further calls for the rest of the abbreviated shift. Pastel used the idle time to consider Murmur's problem. It was wiser than dwelling on his own, until he was in private. So Murmur needed to devise a suitable 'skin' to use while vacationing on the islands. The 'skin', Pastel knew, would have to be morphable into any species that the wearer would like to assume. He resolved to discuss the subject with Zephyr once the shift was over.

Save it for next course, Zephyr directed, in private mode. *It will be mostly technical stuff, anyway.*

Pastel tried to hide his relief. *No nasty surprises?*

Depends how complacent you 'kids' become, Zephyr warned.

Pastel imaged a nervous gulp. *We'll keep that in mind. So, when is the next course?*

Zephyr snorted – this time for all those taking his tutelage to 'hear'. *Since you aren't getting much of a work-out on the Helpline, your last course will begin after you've had a chance to inform your friends and mates.*

Will we be embodied and on the island again? Pastel asked.

As usual, Zephyr was unwilling to commit himself. *We will start off there, anyway.*

Great.

The enigmatic feeling Pastel picked up before Zephyr closed off caused him a few moments of worry, but nothing compared to the weight of his own dilemma. He relocated to a vacant patch of nonspace to think.

The final course; somehow, Pastel had expected to have more time before he'd leave his friends and the Helpline forever.

But maybe it was better this way. He risked getting too deeply involved in the islands project and especially, too chummy with Murmur. He could not afford to let her realize the depth of his feelings for her.

Pastel resolutely turned his attention to how he would function once he was a permanent resident of Earth. Presumably, he could embodying himself again and again, as need be. At least, that's what Zephyr had intimated they would be taught to do. Even if Pastel retained memory of where he came from, total immersion in time-space should soon make it pale into insignificance. And in his endless quest for intimacy, he might one day even share love with an outfocused persona of Murmur. The thought warmed him in places he had never felt before.

The arrival of a couple of beings he didn't know pulled Pastel out of his ruminations. Before Zephyr called him to report for training, he wanted a chance to say goodbye to Whisper and Sirene. It bothered him, of course, knowing they would think he was just going off to class. He would miss them a lot.

With a sigh, he located the mind prints of his friends and joined them.

*

"We're losing him, Zephyr," Murmur said tensely. "I can feel it. He doesn't intend to return."

Despite the energy infusion, the elder looked tired. "We have not lost him yet. I have one more chance to bolster his self-esteem. That's the crux of the problem."

"I know. I've tried, but I can't get through. Let me come along on this course," she pleaded. "Maybe I can do something, help in some way."

Zephyr oozed reluctance. "I don't think it's a good idea. For one thing, coming in at the end like that would look suspicious. He'd know that we know, and that would just make things worse."

"You could say I need to learn how to embody our island vacationers, which is true," she pointed out. "Pastel knows I've been wrestling with it."

"There's someone else to consider: you." Zephyr touched her aura where her heart would have been, had she been in human form. "Your emotions; how you feel about him. Knowing he's gone would be hard on you, but not nearly as tough as watching him leave."

"You're right, but it's worth the risk. *Pastel* is worth the risk." Murmur looked up at Zephyr, resolve streaking through her aura like a lightning storm. "For the second time, I'm going to beg you: Let me come."

CHAPTER 12

So that's what Zephyr was up to, Pastel frowned.

The tropical island was the same, but *they* sure weren't. He looked down at his middle-aged obese belly in dismay. Even that was hard to do with the puffy sacks under his eyes. Gone was most of his hair and, when he spoke, his pleasant baritone voice came out a half-octave higher.

None of Pastel's companions had fared any better. Never before had Pastel seen such a conclave of ugliness. But that was not the only surprise.

Murmur is here to learn how to embody visitors to her islands, Zephyr stated in their public minds, right on cue. Not for the first time, Pastel wondered how their instructor always seemed to know what he was thinking, yet had not picked up on his intentions to defect. Had Pastel successfully buried those thoughts deep enough, then?

Meanwhile, his colleagues – all except Murmur – had turned accusatory eyes on Zephyr, who remained in his sage-wizard embodiment. If anything, he looked even better – younger and more vibrant.

"Ha. Ha. Very amusing," Faire growled. "Now, would you kindly give us back our old bodies?"

Zephyr appeared disgustingly pleased with himself. "Why? Those are perfectly functional."

"They're hideous," Faire fumed. "And I've got to work with this lot. Look at them – *if* you can." He regarded his own scrawny reflection in the large full-length mirror Zephyr had 'thoughtfully' provided for them. "And I'm the most grotesque of the bunch!"

"You don't like what I gave you? Then change it. First one who succeeds teaches the rest." With that, Zephyr disappeared.

"*Now* where did he go?" Serendipity whined.

Fire growled. "Don't bother looking. Knowing him, it's somewhere we can't follow. Of all the lousy tricks."

Faire's weak chin protruded in petulant belligerence. "Well, I don't know about you guys, but *I'm* gonna search this bloody island till I find him."

"And what?" Pastel asked. "He's told us what our task is, impossible though it sounds. He's not likely to change his mind even if you *could* track him down."

Faire's shoulders sagged. "I suppose not. Damn him, anyway."

Pastel sat down heavily on a rock. With all his extra padding, he barely noticed the sharp protrusion on one side. "We're on our own. And we have an assignment."

"And plenty of motivation to do it," Serendipity added, surveying her sagging breasts in contempt. Zephyr had also left them buck naked.

Faire looked beseechingly at the group. "So, how do we change these?"

Pastel reexamined the one pertinent experience they had to draw upon. "Last time, we lightened ourselves so we could fly. That was a body change of sorts, wasn't it?"

"You're talking about rearranging these abominations." Fire was knock-kneed and pigeon-toed with ungainly, oversized feet and ears to match. "Why not just replace them with our former bodies?"

That, of course, would be the preferred choice, Pastel knew. "So, how do we do that?"

"Beats me," Fire admitted. "But if Zephyr can whup us all up bodies and project us into them – all nine of us at once – surely we can learn to do the same for just our own self."

Memory nodded, as she regarded her rake-thin, flat-chested frame with distaste. "You'd think so, wouldn't you? Should we work together or on each other? Or alone, on ourselves?"

No one seemed to have a strong opinion about even that.

After an awkward pause during which the students morosely contemplated their options, Pastel said, "Think I'll just go somewhere and give it some thought. We can't do anything without a plan." Or probably even *with* one, he thought. But anything was better than just standing here looking at the others. They were giving him an eye-ache.

"You're no beauty yourself, you know," Serendipity shot back, as Pastel walked away.

No offense, Pastel replied. He wished they would stay out of his head.

Pastel chose the cave as his lair. From here, he had a fine view of the ocean and no distractions. He settled himself down, resting his back against a rock which jutted out from the wall on his right.

This is what I want to learn, Pastel reminded himself. Not that he'd expected the lesson to take such a bizarre twist. But then, the one constant with Zephyr was the unexpected.

Pastel allowed his mind to wander. It was much like watching a hound dog sniff around for a scent. Pastel would track it down, if there was anything to find. And there must be, since Zephyr could do it so effortlessly . . .

"Pastel!", someone called insistently and, it seemed to him, with some annoyance.

"Wha-?"

"Wake up, you lazy lout! This is no time to goof off." Fire prodded Pastel's backside with his foot.

"Oops." Pastel brought his eyes into focus. How long had he been asleep? Apparently, letting his mind wander wasn't the best approach. Maybe what he needed was activity to get his juices flowing. A nice, invigorating swim should do the trick. Although, butterball that he was, he'd probably float like a cork.

As he headed for the ocean, Pastel decided to check with his classmates, just in case. *Did any of you come up with anything while I was, um, resting my eyes?*

Yeah, right, Fire snorted derisively.

Fire might have been referring to their nonexistent progress or to Pastel's 'just resting' gambit, but his ill temper and homely body graphically answered Pastel's question.

I'm going for a fast swim, Pastel transmitted. *Anyone care to join me?*

Multiple affirmatives flooded in, so Pastel awaited their arrival, even though it took a while.

"Bet I'll sink like a stone." Memory surveyed the ocean gloomily. "I haven't been this skinny since I timespaced as an anorexic. Never thought I'd go through *that* again."

Pastel patted her bony arm. "You aren't. That was just a matter of perception, remember? This isn't . . ." Pastel stopped so abruptly that rotund Murmur bounced off him.

"Hey!" she objected.

Pastel whirled around to face them, almost giddy with excitement. "Did you hear what I said?"

Memory shrugged. "You said anorexia is a matter of perception. I know that now; I didn't then."

"No, he's right," Echo stepped forward, eyes bright with understanding. "*It's all* a matter of perception. And Zephyr just reminded us to watch for that when we were on the Helpline, not two hours ago, the sneaky bugger." Echo's overly-thin lips stretched into a rueful half-smile. "I think he was giving us a hint."

Introspect managed to nod all of her multiple chins at once. "Maybe we should listen more carefully."

"Okay," Pastel said, trying to marshal his thoughts amid the general commentary going on around him. "Let's go on the premise that it's a matter of perception. Which is? Revising our present body, or creating a new one? I would assume the former."

"Likewise," Echo added in a squeaky, falsetto voice. "To fly, we had to 'think' ourselves lighter. But now we have to change our perception of how our body appears to us and to each other."

Introspect raised a chubby finger in caution. "And the longer we look like this, the more we'll relate to ourselves this way. I'd say, don't even look – at ourselves or each other."

"Right you are," Echo continued the thought progression. "Instead, let's picture ourselves as we were in our other body." He turned toward Pastel, then remembered and averted his eyes. "Pastel, you spent an extra course in yours, so you should relate to it most."

In other words, I should have a better chance of succeeding, Pastel mentally translated the inference. And perhaps Echo was right.

"Let's swim first. I want to build up a head of steam, energy-wise." Pastel waded into the warm water until he was waist-deep before launching himself forward on his belly. With the heavy paunch below him, Pastel found swimming was not the delight he remembered it to be. In fact, it had become something of a chore. Pastel gracelessly plowed through the water to release the adrenaline flow he hoped would help. His companions followed him in, many complaining bitterly as they tried to force their imperfect shape to perform as smoothly as its predecessor had.

At last, chest heaving with exertion, Pastel waded back to the beach. He bent over, hands braced on his knees as he tried to catch his breath.

Soon afterwards, Fire and Echo joined him, also puffing.

"Well, wasn't *that* fun?" Fire remarked acidly. He had just tripped over his own feet as he stumbled ashore.

Pastel grimaced. "Look, I'm no happier about this than you are, but now that I'm revved up –"

"I'm just pooped out," Introspect admitted.

"– I intend to put it to good use." Pastel concentrated a few seconds, and managed to moderate his racing heart. "Let's get back to basics. We know how to make ourselves lighter and fly, so I'm starting with that."

There was considerably more of him to lighten than before, but eventually, Pastel was able to lift off the ground and circle the beach. He felt as ungainly as a goony bird coming in for a landing. Most of his colleagues were some distance behind, but he ignored them and veered off around the curve of the island to practice in private. There he came to a halt in mid-air.

If I can lighten myself, I can streamline my belly, Pastel reasoned. He brought up the image of his former sleek, hard-muscled abdomen, using the weight-to-elevating ratio as an indicator rather than looking down at his paunch. It took a lot longer and more concentration than he had expected, but eventually he began to rise.

Encouraged by the minor success, Pastel sharpened the mental image of his present body, imagining it reshaping, becoming ever lighter and, at the same time, stronger and slimmer. Now he was rising more quickly. Pastel came to a stop and risked a peek.

His paunch was almost gone, replaced by what looked like solid muscle. But he still had to look over the bags under his eyes. Also, his hand confirmed, he still had a bald dome.

I shouldn't have to do this piecemeal. Pastel conjured up a vision of his old body, refusing to look at himself until it was so perceptually real in his mind's eye that he felt he could do no better. When he opened his eyes, meaning to check how close to that image he had become, Pastel found himself staring at that body, floating a hand's-breadth away.

"AAAAH!" Pastel cried, startled. He began to plummet, and so did the vacant body.

"I've got you both," a calm, amused voice stated from below.

Both bodies were lowered sedately to the ground until Pastel was at eye-level with his instructor.

"Well done," Zephyr acknowledged. "Although I would remind you to remain in control, no matter what takes you by surprise."

"Thanks." Pastel tried not to show how flustered he felt by the close call. He had been at least sixty feet off the ground.

"You're welcome," Zephyr nodded. "You might also choose a perceptually safer locale than mid-air for developing new technologies."

"I'll keep that in mind." Pastel regarded the empty body beside him. "How do I get out of this and into that?"

"One thing at a time. First, I want you to teach this part to the others. Then we'll tackle trans-embodiment."

Just then, Faire and Serendipity rounded the curve of the island, flying side-by-side.

Zephyr is back! Faire announced with such obvious relief that both Zephyr and Pastel grinned.

"But –" Serendipity stared from Pastel as he currently appeared to his former embodiment. She hovered uncertainly, and looked at Zephyr for explanation.

Zephyr raised a hand. "Wait till the others arrive." *Join us,* he transmitted to the rest of the group, adding an image of their location.

Mutely, Serendipity and Faire lowered themselves onto the beach to wait. Two minutes later, the rest of the 'flock' arrived. All seemed as disconcerted by the presence of two Pastels as Serendipity had been. Pastel remained stock-still, enjoying the effect he was having on his classmates.

"Which one is Pastel?" Memory asked.

Zephyr gave her a look of reproach. "Neither. But if you're wondering which body Pastel *appears* to be occupying . . ." He paused to let the distinction sink in. "It's this one." Zephyr placed a hand on Pastel's shoulder, and Pastel smiled, relaxing his rigid stance. "I have asked him to teach you his technique."

"His?" Echo pounced on the pronoun.

"Yes, mine. Now, if you'll follow me, please." Pastel hovered two feet off the ground, and waited for 'his' students to do the same.

*

"Now you know everything I know," Pastel declared some time later, as they stood beside their preferred bodies.

Zephyr inspected their handiwork. "Not bad. Not bad at all."

"But how do we get out of these and into them?" Fire wanted to know.

Zephyr shook his head. "Listen, people. You can't change *anything* unless you get the facts straight." He ticked them off on his fingers. "Number one: 'You' aren't *in* a body, and you won't be transferring *into* another body. You only *perceive* yourselves as being on this island. You, me, all of us are still in our Native Realm, which is all that there is, no matter how many play worlds or pretend-universes we build."

Fire stirred uneasily. "I know, but –"

Zephyr cut him off. "Two: Transferring into or out of a *perception* of a body occurs from where we really are and never left."

In an instant, Pastel and its colleagues were their normal selves in nonspace, observing their 18 bodies plus Zephyr's on the island.

"When you focus from here, you feel like you're here," Zephyr spoke as though he was teaching novices. "When you project your focus there, you feel like you're there. But the source of that projection is always here, and never leaves here. You can't get away from here no matter what you do *because here is all that there is.* Everything else is make-believe. Or had you forgotten?"

Pastel gulped, blushing furiously. He ducked behind Echo, hoping no one would notice. For the purpose of the course,

Zephyr had embodied their entirety – or so Pastel had surmised. He had been counting heavily on that to ensure he could remove all of himself from their Native Realm.

"Umm, if you're embodying all of our essence when we're over there," Pastel asked, willing his aura to assume a more natural color. "Who's here to focus us there?"

"I am, of course," Zephyr said with aplomb.

Which meant, no matter what, Pastel would have to leave a portion of himself in non-space.

Serendipity gawked at Zephyr, leaking disbelief. "*You* outfocused all of us? At the same time?"

Their instructor imaged a nod. "Simple case of multitasking which, I might add, is a prerequisite if any of you plan on becoming a psyche one day."

Pastel barely heard the exchange. He was thinking about that wretched part of himself he'd have to leave behind. It would have no life at all. But how much of his essence must he sacrifice?

"So to change body – well, pseudo-body, all we have to do is return our focus here and then refocus into the other pseudo-body?", Fire was asking Zephyr.

"How else would you expect to do it?"

Rallying somewhat, Pastel said, "Mind if I try?"

"That's what we're here for."

Echo projected a frown. "Then why do the psyches always send us, if instructors can do it, too?"

"Because until now, there have been too few instructors. We couldn't be spared from teaching and 'eldering' the Helpline to outfocus those who want to go. However, psyches multitask as a matter of course, so it doesn't infringe on their other activities. And outfocusing your student teachers will be part of your job, like I did with you. That's why you're learning it now." Zephyr nodded toward the bodies. "Go ahead, Pastel. Just keep the facts in mind."

Pastel regarded the bodies uncertainly. He would have preferred to try this without an audience. As it was, he had the group's undivided attention.

Just ignore them, Zephyr instructed privately. *Project your focus there and you can go swimming.*

An enticing thought. His body of choice waited quietly; all Pastel had to do was join with it, become one with it.

Pastel could vividly remember what it had felt like to perceptually be in that body – to climb the hill and swim, the exhilaration of flying free as the breeze . . .

"Yikes!" Pastel suddenly found himself in midair, headed straight for a palm tree. He swerved sharply to the left, then shot upward, climbing steeply to avoid plowing into the side of the hill. Next time, he'd better not think of flying when he wanted to project his focus somewhere.

Pastel banked toward the ocean and landed gently a few feet from the water. He glanced back to see if any of his fellow students had followed him 'in' yet, but the other bodies remained motionless. A quick check of the area confirmed no aquatic nasties were around, so Pastel shucked his clothes and dove in.

I've got the island all to myself, he thought, leisurely slicing the water with his hands.

"Hey, you gonna swim all day?" Fire yelled some time later.

Pastel turned in the direction of the voice, and began treading water. "That depends. You coming?"

Fire cast a longing glance toward the cave. "Yeah, I suppose so." He loped toward Pastel just as a whoop of delight heralded the arrival of Whimsy.

One by one, over the next half-hour, the others activated their body of choice and waded into the ocean. Even Zephyr deigned to join them for a while.

At last, Pastel had had enough and headed for the beach.

"Dry yourself off," Zephyr called after him. "And the rest of you do the same. We've got work to do."

No one objected, having had a good, long frolic.

Once again, Pastel noticed, he had become the center of attention. The others were watching to see how he would dry himself off. Next time, he'd make sure he wasn't the first at anything. It turned out to be a lot easier than trans-embodiment, and his colleagues quickly followed suit.

"Assemble by the rock. Like this." Their instructor vanished, to reappear on

'Zephyr's Rock' an instant later. Arms crossed, he waited expectantly.

Faire planted his fists on his hips, glaring balefully towards Zephyr. "Now he expects us to *teleport*?"

"It shouldn't be much different than getting dry," Echo reasoned.

Pastel kept very still, to not distract his colleague.

"Why am I still here?" Echo wondered aloud, after a minute had passed.

"Let's all try," Pastel suggested. "But make sure we choose a different spot to land." He transmitted to them his planned location, shut his eyes and projected his body there. But when he checked, he was still in the same spot, as were the others.

"Did you use the trans-embodiment format?" Serendipity asked. They all agreed that they had.

Fire scowled. "Then why didn't it work?"

Echo reviewed the process. "We projected our focus into these pseudo-bodies, so we should be able to move them . . ." His voice trailed off and he gave Whimsy, who was beside him, a sheepish grin.

Whimsy smiled back. "Just what I was thinking."

"What?" Pastel asked.

"We're all still trying to move these bodies, with us inside them."

It was Pastel's turn to feel silly. "Oh, right." By the looks on the others' faces they, too, recognized the error. "We have to do it from 'home'."

"Care to demonstrate?" Pastel asked.

In response, Whimsy disappeared, to stand and wave from her perch beside Zephyr. One by one in quick succession, the group assembled by the Rock.

"Took you guys long enough," Zephyr grumbled, but he couldn't quite hide the approval in his eyes.

"Full points to Echo and Whimsy," Pastel stated. "They figured it out."

Zephyr inclined his head toward the them. "In that case, Whimsy, you lead."

Her smile vanished.

"Just at Follow the Leader," he said, looking mildly aggrieved. "Boy, you're a suspicious lot."

"With you around, you'd better believe it," Fire said hotly. It was evident he hadn't forgiven Zephyr for scaring the wits out of him the lesson before.

Zephyr didn't look the least repentant for his techniques or for his choice of expressions as he said, "You've had your 'trial by Fire'. There will be no further shocks to your fragile little systems. You have my word."

Fire snorted, but said nothing.

"Whimsy, I want you to teleport your *self* —" Zephyr paused to make sure they all felt the dig. "— about ten feet in the air, just off that rock face over there." He pointed to the cliff wall before turning back to the others. "The rest of you join her there, *one at a time,* where there is a vacant spot. Once you're all assembled, Whimsy will make the next 'jump', or flight or whatever." He turned back to Memory. "Be creative, but be precise and careful. That goes for all of you. Teleporting into a spot occupied by someone else can have uncomfortable repercussions." Zephyr used his thumb to point backhandedly at the cliff wall. "Go."

Obediently, Whimsy disappeared, to hover a hand's-breadth from the wall.

"Fire."

He ended up a good six feet seaward from her and almost a foot above.

Pastel was fourth to go, joining the others lined up outward from Whimsy. Once the whole class was assembled, Whimsy nodded to indicate she was ready to go, and elevated herself before banking toward the ocean.

It didn't take them long to get in the swing of the game. Whimsy impressed Pastel with her imaginative variations on the skills they had learned. She had them fly a figure-8 backwards, then teleport backward and upside down, using memory of their location as their only visual cue.

When Whimsy started running out of maneuvers, Zephyr signaled to Fire, who was next in line, to take the lead. Fire, it turned out, had a few new twists of his own.

Pastel's turn arrived before he had thought out what he would do. It had taken all his concentration to follow the other leaders.

Change body, Zephyr instructed him privately.

Pastel grinned. No wonder the others had come up with so many tactics; they were being coached.

Leaving 'his' body standing with the others on the beach, Pastel mentally became the ugly body, and lifted the rotund, ungainly mass off the ground. A bit of chaos ensued, as each student scrambled to trans-embody themselves and join Pastel in a loop-the-loop.

The delay gave him time to come up with his next gambit. Pastel expanded his mind as much as he could, then split his focus, projecting the other portion as his former body. Hovering in one, he brought the other alongside. The two hims saluted each other.

Introspect gave Pastel a look that said as plain as words he was a major show-off.

Pastel waited, but no new bodies joined them. When it became apparent that none would, both Pastels lowered themselves to the ground.

"That's cheating," Introspect said. "A psyche taught you to split – properly, at any rate. No one taught us."

Belatedly, Pastel realized she was right. In the spirit of the moment, he'd forgotten where he had learned that particular skill. "Sorry. Want to learn?"

Before anyone could accept or pass, Zephyr projected his voice across the distance. "Your answer is 'yes'."

So once again Pastel was put on the spot, and again he had brought it upon himself. But after a grueling half-hour, Pastel wasn't sure he would have been cut out to be a teacher, even if he had intended to stay. Murmur, Introspect, Whimsy and Echo had eventually succeeded in splitting and double-embodying, but nothing Pastel said or did got through to the others. He was sweating profusely, and the students who had been unsuccessful were looking daggers at him. Finally, Zephyr intervened.

"Not everyone can double-embody at this stage. Nor would you need to, as an instructor." Zephyr gestured toward those who were double-embodied. "Rejoin now, please."

It was a relief to reunite as one focus. It was definitely not a trick Pastel intended to make a habit of doing.

"I wouldn't want to do that too often," Echo voiced Pastel's sentiment, as his 'ugly' body froze in place.

"Well, at least you *could*," Fire fumed.

Introspect rolled her shoulders after combining. "Yes, but how often are we likely to need to?"

"She's right, you know," Pastel agreed, anxious to avoid hard feelings. "It's not much more than a party trick." In reality, he could think of a number of potential uses, but he wasn't about to admit it with Fire smoldering the way he was.

Zephyr clapped his hands to get their attention. "Alright, folks. Gather around." He waited till they had done so before heaving an extravagant sigh. "I'm bored. I miss the amenities to which a being of my stature should be accustomed."

That generated a few snickers, but Zephyr raised a hand. "No, I'm serious." He pointed to the area, a hundred yards away, where the beach widened and flattened out somewhat. "I would like a chateau of my own there. Nothing too elaborate. A three-story, seven-bedroom mansion with a garage to one side large enough to house six cars should do me fine, Pastel and Murmur. Take turns instructing your partner on how to build the different portions, but I want it ready for me to move into by sundown."

Pastel didn't know whether to laugh or be indignant. "You expect us to build it for you?"

"Only if you insist on doing it the hard way."

"Oh, right."

But Zephyr's grandiose plans were just beginning. "Serendipity and Introspect, I envision an English-style flower garden with shrubs and hedges all around the estate, with an abundance of appropriate walkways. And remove that hill, while you're at it; it's blocking my view."

"Yes, Master," Serendipity bowed low in mock servitude.

"Can I work with Serendipity?" Faire piped up. "We make a great team. Uh, and I like flowers."

Zephyr glared at him. "I *know* how you two team up. She might not appreciate you calling that 'work'."

Faire's cheeks flushed, while the others enjoyed a hearty laugh at his expense. Evidently, Zephyr had been fully aware of their liaisons.

"No," their instructor ruled. "I think you and Fire will have your hands full making my Olympic-size swimming pool and then filling it with fresh water."

"Where are we supposed to get —" Faire's voice trailed off. "Forget I asked that."

Zephyr was already turning away from Faire. "Now, Memory, Echo and Whimsy, that garage will look awfully bare without a fleet of expensive classic cars in it. As will the runway I want you to build over yonder for the executive jet Fire and Faire will also whip up for me." Zephyr laced his fingers and cracked his knuckles backward. "All this planning has tuckered me out. Time for a nap." With that, he vanished.

"Think anyone would notice – or even care – if he disappeared from nonspace entirely?" Fire asked with a nasty grin.

"I heard that!" The disembodied voice seemed to be coming from everywhere at once. "Quit griping and get to work. You can have your own students build you anything you want, if you learn this right."

"Hmm. Hadn't thought of that." Fire regarded their patch of beach with a critical eye. "But I'll need a much bigger island for my theme park."

Pastel didn't catch Faire's reply as the two walked away. Murmur joined Pastel in flight to the site of Zephyr's proposed mansion. They landed, backs to the ocean.

"Think we can create it all at once?" She eyed the beach doubtfully.

"I can't; that much I know. Care to try?"

She pursed her lips. "Nope."

Murmur imaged the sand level and edged it on the seaward side with a rock-and-mortar retaining wall. After she had materialized a thin, sharp-pointed stick, Murmur drew a huge rectangle in the sand. "Here's what I want the foundation to look like:"

*

Pastel was find it increasingly difficult to concentrate on their task, now that it was nearly complete. It was almost time for him to leave. His mind was already casting about for a suitable place on Earth to lay low until the others returned to the Native Realm. A sudden tension in Murmur's stance garnered his attention.

"What's wrong?" Pastel asked.

She had just finish 'laying' the carpet throughout the downstairs, except for the kitchen and bathrooms. The shade was just a tad off what he had visualized for her to create, but not enough to be worth while mentioning. Why was she looking upset?

Murmur opened her mouth to speak, but nothing came out.

Excuse us, Pastel, Zephyr transmitted.

An instant later, Murmur was standing a fair distance down the beach, where Zephyr had just appeared. They seemed to be having an intense conversation, if the expression on Murmur's face was any indication. While Pastel put the finishing touches to the mansion, he considered how little of his essence he would have to move back into nonspace. No one was paying him the least bit of attention. A few more minutes and he would be finished here, in more ways than one. When he teleported himself away, everyone would just think he was inside the house. By the time they knew what had happened, he'd be long gone. His only regret was that he couldn't say goodbye to Murmur.

*

"What did you do that for?" Murmur demanded, desperate to get back to Pastel. "He's about to leave. This is my last chance to talk him out of it."

Zephyr shook his head sadly. "The psyches themselves reminded me that we must not interfere with his choices. I'm sorry, but I did warn you this might happen."

Murmur filled her lungs. "Well, at least," she bellowed loud enough that Pastel couldn't fail to hear. "Let me tell the stupid son-of-a-bitch I love him."

Before Zephyr could stop her, Murmur teleported in front of an astonished Pastel, grabbed his head with both hands and planted a ferocious kiss on his lips.

"There! Now you know. Deal with it!" she roared.

Projects finished? Zephyr transmitted.

*

Pastel gawked at Murmur, unable to believe the evidence of his ears or lips. She loved *him?* How could that be? His mind dispassionately reviewed the moment and dubbed it false, an illusion. Dimly, Pastel registered Zephyr's telepathic query and Murmur's reply. And then they were gone – creations and all.

Pastel lurched forward, jolted out of his torpor.

"MURMUR!" His outstretched hand pawed the spot where she had been a scant moment ago. "No! Oh, please, no! Come back," he shouted. But it was too late.

That was when the truth hit him with the force of an atom bomb. Pastel hadn't defected; he'd been exiled.

CHAPTER 13

Like an unwanted fetus ripped from its mother's womb, Pastel felt his life force bleed away as he fell heavily to the sand. At the same time, his massive mind withered and shrunk till he doubted he could form a single coherent thought. Wave upon wave of life and consciousness flowed from his body. Pastel writhed with the sheer physical and emotional horror of being so swiftly and drastically depleted. On and on it went, until Pastel felt he must surely die. When at last the energy hemorrhage stopped, the tears began, and Pastel imploded into a black hole of despair.

Congratulations, fool, his subconscious mocked him. *You got what you wanted and just what you deserve: you're human. And all it cost you was your home and soulmate. Bravo!*

Pastel rocked in anguish, ragged sobs wrenching at his throat. At long last, he had found love, only to lose it, and he had no one to blame but himself.

You betrayed everyone you knew, everyone who cared for you and trusted you, his subconscious continued. *Murmur, Zephyr, Whisper, all the students you were supposed to teach; students that are needed because of* your *unconsidered, self-motivated project.*

Time fell away under the lashes of the damning diatribe. Pastel curled in a fetal position, accepting it without debate, knowing that every word was true. No torture he had ever endured in any lifetime could match the agony of his self-conflagration. At last, the inner voice went silent, and Pastel, too exhausted to think or feel any more, slipped mercifully into sleep.

*

Wavelets licking at his feet awakened him long after sunset. Pastel sat up and looked around, disoriented. And then he remembered. A ragged whimper escaped from deep within, causing him to wince. His throat felt like brittle parchment, and his stomach roiled ominously. He was human, alright. Which meant he would need sustenance to survive.

The thought brought Pastel out of his self-absorption. If he was to find food and water tonight, he had very little time to do so before full nightfall. A glance at the heavens afforded one boon: there would be an almost full moon to help guide his steps, should he need it.

Pastel remembered seeing a few mango-laden trees partway up the hill on the other side, and nearby a fresh-water spring had trickled over a rock face. He lurched to his feet and broke into an ungainly run. There was no point trying to fly or teleport; Zephyr would have stripped him of those skills along with his immortality – and rightly so. Had he been in Zephyr's shoes, Pastel suspected he would have removed all sustenance and left the traitor to die.

But when he arrived, just as the last dregs of light was leaching from the horizon, there were the spring and fruit, right where he remembered seeing them. As the water trickled down his parched throat, Pastel silently thanked Zephyr for that mercy. He collected six mangoes and used the moonlight to follow the curving beach to 'Zephyr's Rock'.

By the time his hunger was assuaged, Pastel was already sick of the view. The surface of the moonlit ocean stretched into infinity: serene, barren and deathly still. Breathtaking beauty in a counterfeit world. And he was the phoniest thing in it.

"Fool, *fool, FOOL!*" Pastel yelled, pounding his fist on the rock. "What the *hell* are you doing here? Murmur loves you. Yeah, *you* – you stupid, pathetic, worthless bastard –"

Pastel froze, lips curled in self-loathing, as he realized the significance of what he was saying: Yes, it was true: He hated himself. And why shouldn't he, after the way he'd behaved?

You will not allow yourself to have or keep what you do not feel you deserve, a psyche had told him not so long ago.

"Well, I *don't* deserve love. I never have and I never will," Pastel bristled, thumping the rock once more for emphasis.

Why not? a tiny voice from within asked, curious rather than forceful.

"Because I don't. Period. I'm just a backstabbing, selfish loser, and Murmur deserves the best. That sure as hell ain't me!"

'If we were perfect, there'd be no room for improvement, would there? Besides, just like Earth, 'heaven' is what you make it,' the inner voice reminded him. *That's what Zephyr told Felicity when she picked up on your thoughts, remember? Anyway, Zephyr just gave you your wish. It was a fulfillment, not a sentence.*

Pastel snorted in derision. "Yeah, right. I pull that kind of treachery on everyone, and they'll just let me waltz back in and welcome me with open arms. Tell me another one!"

Technically, you didn't defect; you were left behind.

Which was true enough. Pastel sat up straight, wondering. Had he been locked out for ever, or was Zephyr just giving him 'time out' to think? But even if Pastel could go back, what made him think Murmur would want him? She had probably just said she loved him to keep him from leaving, right? Right . . .?

He listened for his inner voice to respond, but this time it was silent.

The moon had reached its zenith before Pastel summoned enough courage to place the call.

"Pastel?", an astonished Fire replied. Obviously, Team 2 was on shift at the moment. "What are you doing there? We got back hours ago, your time."

"Uh, it's a long story. Can you 'path Zephyr for me, please?"

"Why?" Fire sounded more confused than annoyed. "Just pop back here and –"

Pastel was perspiring, but he wrestled his emotions under control. He had no desire to play 'true confessions' with Fire. "I'll explain later, okay? Can you just get Zephyr for me?"

"Alright. Hang on."

During the prolonged silence which followed, Pastel took a bath in his own sweat. Zephyr was not going to take his call; he was certain of it. Panic was setting in by the time the familiar voice appeared in Pastel's mind.

"Bored so soon?"

Pastel's mouth worked, but so many words were vying to be voiced that nothing came out. His Adam's apple bounced like a bobber with a fish on the line. What could he *possibly* say?

"Feeling a tad sheepish, are we?" Zephyr needled. Surprisingly, there was no rancor to the question.

At last, Pastel found his voice. "After what I did? – well, would have done, if you hadn't beat me to it. That was the scummiest, backstabbingest . . ." He cast about for words to describe the depth of his crime and failed.

"Did you expect otherwise?"

The question took Pastel by surprise. "What do you mean?"

Zephyr conjured a shrug. "You tell me: What do you get when you combine low self-esteem with love you can't live without but sanctimoniously reject?"

"Um, irrational behavior?"

"At first, yes. But in the end the result is always the same – always: It devolves into warped, heinous expressions of bastardized adoration. The genuine love becomes deified. Over time, in its name, no behavior is too despicable, no atrocity too base to be rejected. What you now perceive as an act of treachery against your true family seemed noble to you, when viewed through that twisted filter, did it not? Madness grows from such delusions."

Pastel nodded, knowing his instructor was right.

"I interfered with your choice by acting on your behalf," Zephyr continued, adding almost conversationally, "Believe me, the psyches were not pleased. But what could they say, really? I, too, had the right to choose how I would handle you. And so, when you return – I rightly assume you want to?"

"Yes, more than anything," Pastel croaked. It seemed a pitifully inadequate response.

"When you return, you will take on the added task of searching the *public* minds of our people. Any who you find heading down the same path you just took, you will befriend and give the benefit of your present experience. Understood?"

Pastel felt like 'Zephyr's Rock' had been lifted off his shoulders. "And how! Zephyr, I am so very sorry –"

"Don't apologize to me. Apologize to her."

*

Pastel found himself standing in front of Murmur. She was squatting alone on the island beach in nonspace, embodied as a comely red-headed female in her early twenties. Sand slipped through her fingers, and her face looked sadder than he would ever have believed possible. She looked up then, and something indiscernible flickered in her eyes.

"Did you mean it?" Pastel blurted out. "Do you really love me?"

"That depends. If I say 'no', will you run?"

Pastel conjured up the body he had worn on the Pacific island and knelt down in front of her. "No. If they don't kick me out for being a total idiot, I'll stay, no matter what. But –". He took her sandy hand in his. "I'll do whatever it takes to become worthy of your love, if you'll let me. *Please* let me try, Murmur. Please love me."

"I do." She squeezed his hand. "And there is only one way to be worthy of love."

Pastel listened with every fiber of his soul. "How?"

"Return it, pure and simple."

He gulped painfully, feeling tears slide down his cheeks. "I will. I do! I love you, Murmur, so incredibly much it hurts."

Then she was in his arms, her lips pressed against his. Pastel felt like a plastic doll miraculously given life. He kissed her with all his being, passion rising in him like a mighty volcano.

And then she was pulling him beneath their Tree. A snap of her fingers dispensed with their clothes.

*

With the pleasures of time-space in their Native Realm, why should our people bother to outfocus? psyche4 expressed its growing concern.

Psyche2 was not in the least worried. *These diversions offer no challenges, no surprises. But they do whet the appetite, and therein lies their value.*

And Pastel?

Psyche2 indulgently overviewed the gyrating human forms locked in coital ecstasy. For once, it deigned to speak in tenses. *When it and its soulmate eventually tire of their mock timespacing games, they and Zephyr will join us on the Board of Directors. And that, colleagues, is when the real fun will begin!*

Excerpts from Pastel's Book of Aphorisms

*(For consistency sake,
the masculine is used throughout.)*

- Fried rice is a dish. So is the bowl in which it is served. But they are quite different, in exactly the same way a human being and the vessel in which he appears are different. Do not confuse content with container.

- Offer someone too much freedom, knowledge or option at one time and he will recoil from it. Any overload is traumatic.

- People automatically keep themselves in the physical, mental, emotional, social and behavioral state they relate to for themselves. To break that standing takes a strong, heartfelt decision backed by some action towards the goal. If they hold to the decision, completion will occur, in time.

341

- If today's crop of events, emotions and reactions are like yesterday's, the person is still running on yesterday's mental/emotional Template.

- Remaining focused on the past is like staring in the rear-view mirror while driving down the road, and will likely produce the same results.

- Duty is a taught perspective which tricks the person into believing duty is more worthy, necessary or important than living his own life. The negative emotions this generates from within proclaim this view to be false, but he has been taught to ignore such input in the name of duty.

- Emotions and feelings hold beliefs in place. The purer and stronger these emotions are, the more people tend to cling to their beliefs and what their emotions are telling them about it.

- The gift of an item or action is just an emotion or feeling in disguise. The emotion/feeling is the true gift.

- Trust is taking for granted the other person's tendency to act in your best interests.

- The human body is part of the person's outer environment (sort of a time-space suit).

- Gentleness is necessary with those who are frail of body, fearful of emotions or uncertain of mind. To be 'sensitive' is to be frail in that area. As such, it is not a quality but a weakness.

- Humility is as unworthy as is arrogance. A humble person does not value himself or acknowledge his strengths. As such, it is a fault.

- Trade what no longer serves your best interests for something which does. Too often, we trade what we value for that which binds, restricts or disappoints us.

- The biggest danger to your well-being is to let a situation or discomfort continue long enough that you accept it as the 'norm'. You are either well or you aren't. You are happy or you aren't. You are progressing or you aren't. And if you aren't, that aspect of you will eventually decay. Your worst enemy is postponing resolution of your problems.

- If you don't like something that seems to have settled in, *get rid of it,* or in due course, it will be you who is forced to leave. *Never* permit any force to evict you! This is your life, your world, your 'session'. You are the one irreplaceable element in it. Without you, it has no purpose. And if you run from it, or let it run you, then you have forgotten *your* purposes.

- Many are bound by their feelings of duty, guilt, fear of what their ward will say if they change the arrangement, and fear of what others would say or think of them for doing so. When all these are present, you can be sure of one thing: love isn't.

- In many cases, a martyr is just a masochist with a cause.

- Wait for a light, and you may wait forever. A vigil is the loneliest, emptiest expression of loyalty, with the person abdicating his right to make decisions.

- Verbal imagery can sometimes pull your mind and feelings away from efforts to achieve your goal. Instead, it presents fanciful, emotionally-charged visions which have nothing to do with reality. A prime example is 'wait for your ship to come in'. That is only valid if you own a ship. However, *you* are your own ship, and you're already here. What do you choose to do with you now?

- Hopes and dreams get you nowhere. Replace them with planning, goals, decisions and action.

- A lifetime is all option and no promise. You provide the promises to yourself and fulfill them.

- Leave nothing to chance; decide.

- Destiny is what a person can expect if he continues on his current path, making no changes along the way.

- "Hear me" now means "Listen to me". "Listen to me" now means "Obey me". Become aware of the real meaning in the things you say and hear.

- People try to unravel the 3-D symbols in their life, as they search for the 'meaning of life'. Life is not a purpose; it is an opportunity to experience one's self as a being being human. *You* give meaning to your lifetime (or don't). Meaning is for you to assign, not to seek 'out there'. What do you 'mean' to do with your life?

- It was an undeniable truth that mankind couldn't fly – until people decided to fly anyway. The moment they succeeded, *that truth became false.* In the end, decisions replace truths and render them false.

- Be grateful that the most abundant waste products – empty words – are biodegradable.

- There are givers, takers, acceptors and sharers.
  A giver gives away what he values.
  A taker draws from others what he values.
  An acceptor must wait to be offered what he values.
  Sharers both receive and provide what they value.

- People are individuals. They have their own paths, their own realities. They cannot live your reality, and you cannot live theirs. You can share realities in perspective, but not in fact.

- Love will live out, for people to see, feel and judge, the hidden properties they have attached to it.

- What people love and hate tells them a lot about themselves.

- Humor can break down hostility and allow the first form of sharing to occur: a smile or a laugh.

- Acknowledge your real motive for what you plan to do or experience, for the results will reflect them.

- There are no wrong decisions, as each decision has a consequence, and each consequence is a lesson. What a person learns from them determines whether he will, in hindsight, label them 'right' or 'wrong'.

- Lessons not learned will be repeated ever more forcefully until you do learn them or they defeat you.

- Salvation occurs when a miserable person acknowledges his present and recognizes his future, then changes his mind.

- Solace does not come from pity or compensation, but from purpose reborn.

- Knowledge is available everywhere. Wisdom comes from within.

- Suffering is the opposite of learning. Once learned in an area, a person will never tolerate suffering there again.

- Work is the human body's staple activity. Play is the imagination's staple self-expression. Both must be in balance for the person's life to run smoothly. The need for creative expression is sadly underplayed (pun intended). Play time gives purpose (reward) to work. Work gives purpose and appreciation to play time.

- Harvest the fruits of your wisdom and ingenuity. Then you won't have to make do with the meager fruits of your labor.

- The heart of any action is the goal it will fulfill.

- Hope is a stillborn goal. Hope is all you have left when you do nothing towards achievement.

- All human achievement was once a figment of the imagination. 'Impossible' is a figment of our beliefs.

- The prize which comes from success is a new set of options previously unavailable to you or unnoticed by you.

- Choose one:
  <u>To age and drain your body</u>:
  - Do not fulfill your needs and desires, nor complete your personal goals.
  - Fulfill the needs and desires of others, and complete goals that aren't yours.
  - Do nothing different that would please or stimulate you. Stagnate.

  Signs: Frustration, anger, boredom, sluggishness, lack of purpose, lack of direction.

  <u>To enliven and energize your body</u>:
  - Do the opposite of 'A'.

  Signs: Enthusiasm, energy, purpose, happy anticipation, achievement, joy, self-satisfaction.

- Attempting to hasten your future best interests often keeps you from noticing the step-by-step learnings that will get you there.

- Personal exploration and progress starts the minute boredom stops feeling safe or comfortable.

- Freedom is always sought and jealously guarded, but it is seldom gainfully employed.

- Bondage forces a person to do the bidding of others. Freedom is a working agreement to change and explore.

- Symbolically, the heart feeds the soul's need to feel and the psyche's need to experience. When the soul and psyche are being nourished, they in turn nurture the human body.

- The soul wants *everything*, and will never settle for less.

- Wisdom frees the soul from attending the humdrum and permits it to express its knowing in an active way in your world.

- Time is neither an ally nor an enemy. It is a platform, as is space. Learn to use your tools, or they will continue to use you.

- No masterpiece is judged by the time it took.

- A most telling societal expectation is that we 'act our age'. Our *bodies* have an age; we who function through them do not.

- Speed up what you don't enjoy that you insist on putting yourself through, and go for quality and enjoyment in what you want to experience and express. Time is *not* a constant; you control it. Make it work for you.

- Humans relate to themselves by gender and call their body 'it'. Yet it is only our time-space body that has gender. We who experience, express and explore through that body have no gender. We are beings, being human.

- Death is neither the end nor beginning; it is a continuation. When you make an abrupt change of experience (such as moving far away), your experience is much like leaving a lifetime. You retain the memories of where you were and why, and of what you experienced there. You feel not-there-anymore – objective rather than immersed – and you have a whole new situation within which to work and to mold to your liking.

- Intuition is knowing what you know, without being able to quote a source. When you are at peace with yourself, you hear your subtle knowings which are otherwise drowned out by the noise of internal conflict.

- Love attracts lovers.
  Joy attracts the exhilarated.
  Facts attract scientists.
  Life attracts lovers of life.
  Freedom attracts the bound.
  Learning attracts the needy.
  We are all 'in need' of one concept or another, and when fulfilled they nourish our soul.

- Self is the most real element of any reality a person will ever perceive, but it is the trickiest to recognize and get to know.

- 'You' do not need to be explained, justified or pitied.

- The wisest person you can ever know is yourself. You have every answer to every question you will ever ask yourself in three-dimensional form. You would not have an experience because you don't know the answer; you would have it to experience the answer. Experience lets you feel what is otherwise only observations or objective data.

354

- A person can always recognize true-self traits in that he does not feel the need to justify them to himself or display them to others.

- Seek the 'truth', and you will find a lie for all seasons.
  Seek the facts, and you will find the building-blocks of understanding.
  Seek understanding, and behind it you will discover purposes.
  Seek purposes, and you will find the motivation to accomplish.
  Seek accomplishments, and you will experience self-worth.
  Seek self-worth, and you will find 'you' waiting and oh-so-happy to at last be discovered by you.
  You seek you. If you do not see you *everywhere,* you have not found who you are yet.

- No matter how much energy a person has stored within him, if it doesn't flow it won't be felt. For the most part, people can only feel change.

- Harbor fears, and they will seek resolution through frightening events. Harbor love, and it will leak out in countless subtle self-expressions. Harbor you, and you will always seek you-know-not-what. Harbor nothing, and you will be you, fully and gainfully expressed.

- When a person accepts imagination, thought and feelings as his natural habitat, he rises above the commonplace. How he uses these tools is his unique personality-print as a timespacer.

- Life properties are not meant to be static. They are meant to be in motion, in use, in action. That is what life is: action. Look at the word: If you divide it in two, you have 'act' and 'ion'. 'Act' is the application of energy. 'Ion' is a form of energy.